HELENA MARÍA VIRAMONTES, author of *The Moths and Other Stories*, was born in East Los Angeles. A community organizer and coordinator of the Los Angeles Latino Writers Association, she has won several literary awards, and her work is widely anthologized. She currently lives in Ithaca, New York, where she is a creative writing professor at Cornell University.

D0018090

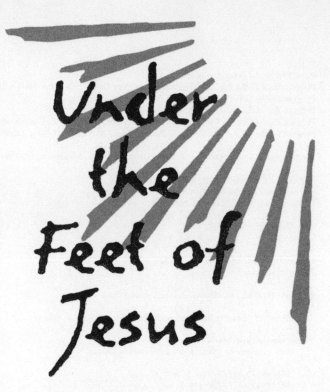

Under the Feet of Jesus

Helena María Viramontes

A PLUME BOOK

PLUME
Published by the Penguin Group
Penguin Books USA Inc., 375 Hudson Street, New York, New York 10014, U.S.A.
Penguin Books Ltd, 27 Wrights Lane, London W8 5TZ, England
Penguin Books Australia Ltd, Ringwood, Victoria, Australia
Penguin Books Canada Ltd, 10 Alcorn Avenue, Toronto, Ontario, Canada M4V 3B2
Penguin Books (N.Z.) Ltd, 182–190 Wairau Road, Auckland 10, New Zealand

Penguin Books Ltd, Registered Offices: Harmondsworth, Middlesex, England

Published by Plume, an imprint of Dutton Signet,
a division of Penguin Books USA Inc.
Previously published in a Dutton edition.

First Plume Printing, April, 1996
40 39 38 37 36 35 34 33 32 31

Ⓟ REGISTERED TRADEMARK—MARCA REGISTRADA

The Library of Congress has catalogued the Dutton edition as follows:

Viramontes, Helena María
    Under the feet of Jesus / Helena María Viramontes.
        p.   cm.
    ISBN 0-525-93949-0 (hc.)
    ISBN 0-452-27387-0 (pbk.)
    I. Title.
PS3572.163U53   1995
813'.54—dc20   94–46860
                                              CIP

Printed in the United States of America
Original hardcover design by Leonard Telesca

PUBLISHER'S NOTE
This is a work of fiction. Names, characters, places, and incidents either are the
products of the author's imagination or are used fictitiously, and any resemblance to
actual persons, living or dead, events, or locales is entirely coincidental.

To my parents

Mary Louise LaBrada Viramontes
and
Serafin Bermúdes Viramontes

who met in Buttonwillow
picking cotton

In Memory of

César Chávez

One

Had they been heading for the barn all along? Estrella didn't know. The barn had burst through a clearing of trees and the cratered roof reminded her of the full moon. They were seven altogether—their belongings weighed down an old Chevy Capri station wagon, the clouds above them ready to burst like cotton plants. Then the barn disappeared into a hillside of brittle bush and opuntia cactus as the man who was not her father maneuvered the wagon through a laborious curve.

Sunlight weaved in and out of the clouds. Wisps of wind ruffled the orange and avocado and peach trees which rolled and tumbled as far back as the etched horizon of the mountain range. A cluster of amputated trees marked the entrance of the side road. The mother said Aquí, and the man whom they called Perfecto slowed down and turned. The mother refolded the Phillips 66 map and shouted that she hoped the winds would push the clouds away and it wouldn't rain. She had to repeat it over the booming muffler to Perfecto and he tested the windshield wipers. One wiper scraped away a splattered insect. He scratched his head and said he was tired of sleeping sitting up in the car. And then they were quiet.

The silence and the barn and the clouds meant many things. It was always a question of work, and work depended on the harvest, the car running, their health, the conditions of the road, how long the money held out, and the weather, which meant they could depend on nothing. Estrella watched Perfecto's hand scratching the back of his head with uncertainty. His skin was like the bark of a juniper tree.

The beige station wagon bumped along the unpaved road, bucking the bundles and the rolled tarpaulin and pipes tied with a web of ropes to the luggage rack.

—Ssshh, hissed Alejo to his cousin, Someone's coming.

—Shit, I hate this.

—Quiet.

Alejo saw the wagon from the tall peach tree in the orchard. He had been picking peaches, ripe from the direct sun, and handed his selections between the rustle of branches to his cousin, Gumecindo, who clutched a flour sack and doubled as a lookout. They labored be-

4

fore sunset, right after work, when others would not see them.

The cousins had argued with one another, first about whose turn it was to climb up the trees, second about a man named Plato. Gumecindo thought Plato was "plate" in gringo Spanish, and when Alejo told him otherwise, they laughed so hard they had to remind themselves of why they were in the peach orchard. Alejo, slender and the more agile of the two, tested the slouching branches for strength, then pulled himself up until the younger branches creaked. Peach fuzz tickled his face.

He picked the brightest peaches until he heard a car engine puckering like marbles against the hood and he hunched into the bushy canopy of the tree. Through the colander of leaves, Alejo watched the car door open, its engine idling, while wasps droned near the resinous fruit. Their hind legs dangled like golden threads.

A wiry man emerged from the station wagon, his creased and baggy trousers hiked above his waist. There was a slick wax shine to the cap of baldness on the thin man's head. Someone from inside the car handed him a hat. He palmed his sparse silver hair, then jammed the hat on his head and then he reached for a rope tied above the car and pulled so that the bundle looked like a belly over a tightened belt. His glasses caught reflections of the afternoon sun as he knotted the rope and he turned towards the peach orchard, right in the direction of Alejo, and the man's glasses glimmered like

5

sparks. Alejo quickly crouched further into the foliage and a branch snapped above his head. He pushed down a few leafy twigs and followed the wagon's tire tread until the dust settled.

Perfecto headed for the clearing and steered away from the potholes but still the car dipped and bumped and the empty water bottle on the dash and coffee cups and sun visors flapped down and the maps spilled onto the mother's lap. Be careful, she scolded, bracing her arm against the sun-cracked dashboard. He wedged the bottle between them. The twin girls startled awake.

—Are we there yet? Ricky asked the mother. He reached up and halted a white plastic rosary which hung from the rearview mirror. Estrella waited for the mother's answer.

Perfecto lifted a finger from the steering wheel and pointed to a shabby wood frame bungalow. Blond tufts of asparagus weeds grew along the front of the bungalow and in between the warped boards of the porch steps.

—Is this it, Petra? he asked.

Petra crossed her arms. The bigger oak tree which once branched an arc of shade to the roof was cut so far down, the stump was useless even as a seat. The cooking pit seemed farther from the porch.

—Gracias a Diós, she answered, and Perfecto cranked the parking brake. The wagon puckered and fell silent.

—We're here? asked Estrella.

6

—We're here, said the mother, Petra.

—We're here, whispered Estrella to her sleeping brother Arnulfo.

The doors sprang open. Stray socks, balls of crushed waxed paper, peanut shells, and a plastic doll tumbled from the car. The twin girls spilled out of the backseat first. Estrella emerged after her brothers, her legs uncurling and her bare toes flexing. She picked up the doll and felt kinks in her back. Ricky had already stepped on it.

—You okay? she asked the naked doll and then she shook the doll's head NO.

—Sure you are, she said and tossed it back on the seat. Estrella ran, her flowered dress billowing, strands of black hair escaping from her unraveling braid. The twins trailed like busy chicks. The boys headed for the vacant corrals. They jumped the wooden fence and ran, jostling the tall grass.

Petra had deep coffee-colored skin and black, kinked hair that she tamed with a short braid. She walked to the cooking pit in flapping rubber sandals, then arched her back. The grate needed scrubbing and she looked around for horsetail weed, which was just as good for scouring as steel wool. With a stick left by the last occupants, she poked the coal and wood ash. The fragrance of toasted corn tortillas, of garlic and chile bubbling over the flames, of fried tripas spitting fat in a cast-iron skillet, rose like dust to her nose. She lifted

the grate, and touched the sticky char. Petra turned
when the porch planks moaned at the weight of Perfecto's boot popping a scorpion.

—Niño de tierra, he said, looking around for any
more. The wind lifted the large rim of his hat.

Perfecto inspected the two-room bungalow, sliding
his thick bifocals up to the bridge of his nose. He rattled
the knob, stepped into a dingy room with a window
facing the porch. The stink of despair shot through the
musty sunlight, and he knocked a fist against the window to loosen the swollen pane to get some fresh air
into the room. Cobwebs laced the corners. There were
no beds and only a few crates used for chairs arranged
around one table as if for a game of cards. Perfecto
figured only men had stayed here. He planned to move
the table outside near the cooking pit. Three crates in
the corner would be a good place to set up Petra's altar
with Jesucristo, La Virgen María y José. He walked
slowly, studying the ceiling for leaks.

In the center of the second room, Perfecto spotted a
dead bird. Birds, the sparrows especially, found their
way into abandoned houses only to bombard themselves against the walls. But dead birds spooked Petra
so he picked the carcass up by its stiff taloned feet, and
dumped it out the side window. Perfecto Flores, who
was thirty-seven years older than Petra, would not men-
tion the bird.

Petra pulled the broom out of the station wagon. She
watched Estrella's long legs leap over the tall blades of

wild mustard grass, her own legs shackled by varicose veins. She called for Estrella and raised a broom as a threat, screamed to her children:

—Get back this minute, huercos fregados, who do you think you are, corriendo sin zapatos? ¡Te van a comer los niños de tierra! Without so much as putting on your shoes, huerquitos fregados! but her words netted in the rustle of the trees.

Estrella listened to the tease of words and leaves. The eucalyptus trees lined the dirt road like a row of thin dancing girls fanning their feathers. The breeze billowed her dress and for a moment she held her elbows as she watched the mother swish the broom against the mentholated wind. Then Estrella looked at the barn way back to the side of the bungalow. She couldn't wait until morning to investigate and began running again. Being the oldest, just turned the corner to thirteen (the mother thought the number unlucky, and they both waited anxiously for her fourteenth birthday), Estrella came upon the barn first. She halted the twins with a shove and rubbed her bare foot against clumps of dandelions to answer an itch.

The children stood in the shade of the barn, a cathedral of a building. The twins' laughter curdled into whispers. The one twin, Perla, became frightened and scratched the divide where her two braids parted. The other twin, who went by Cookie though her name was Cuca, closed an eye and her gaze followed the slanted, splintery wood sheeting until she was staring at the glaring sky. Only Estrella studied the door with its flaked white paint, holding fast to keep the torn hem of her dress from fanning up with the wind.

Perla stopped scratching. She waited to see what her eldest sister would do.

—I'll tell Mama, Cookie dared.

Estrella offered her head first. The scent of dung and damp hay lingered thick and the motes of dust swirled. The barn seemed so strangely vacant; the absence clung heavy and the wind whistled between the planks. She noticed a chain suspended from the ceiling. Thick-linked, long and rusty, it swayed like a pendulum, as if someone had just touched it and ran off.

The barn door suddenly swung loose, squeaking worse than the brakes on Perfecto's wagon. The screech of the rusted hinge flushed out the owls and swallows roosting in the gable, a riot of feathers and fluttering that startled the twins. It happened so quickly. The swallows and owls shrieking in a burst of furious flight, feathers snowing down, the girls screaming.

—Cats fighting. Alejo whispered between the toes of his Concord tennis shoes, through the branches and down to Gumecindo. Then the cousins looked up. Birds whirled like frantic bits of torn paper. The many rows of trees whipped, then paused, then whipped again, and Alejo couldn't read which direction the birds came from. A few peaches thudded on the ground. Alejo clasped a branch and as he climbed down, a gnarled limb bristled against his spine. It chilled him. His feet dangled and he dropped to the ground, dust rising from beneath his shoes.

—Let's get outta here, Gumecindo pleaded. He dragged a full sack to a tree and leaned it against the trunk. He flipped his head back to see what Alejo would do. The screaming halted as abruptly as it had started. A few stray birds glided by. What do you think?

—It's just cats fighting, Alejo repeated, more for himself than for his cousin. Daylight was waning. He inspected the trees to the south of him, the peaches lush and ready. The remaining sunlight lit the top of the trees; the leaves flickered like gold licks of fire. He grabbed one ear of the cloth sack held by Gumecindo, then grabbed the other sack from the tree and weighed the two, his hands like scales to make sure they both had equal shares. He passed the bigger, bulkier sack to a frightened Gumecindo.

—I always thought La Llorona was just a story, Gumecindo said. His shadow was long and split by a trunk and for a moment Alejo thought it odd the way the head of his cousin's shadow kept smashing into the trees as they walked. Distracted, Alejo tripped on a root and the peaches rolled out. The two young men began picking up the fruit, the lace of shadowed leaves on their backs.

—Just a few more trees before the dark hits, okay 'mano? Alejo asked, throwing some of the selected peaches away. Half of these are going to bruise.

—Shit, I hate this.

—Nobody buys fruit with bruises.

—Ask me if I care.

What Estrella remembered most of her real father was an orange. He had peeled a huge orange for her in an orchard where they stopped to pee. They were traveling north where the raisin grapes were ready for sun drying and the work was said to be plentiful. The twins wore diapers then, babies whose fists punched the air with hysteria. The boys managed to relieve themselves without ceremony by the side of the pickup, while Estrella and the mother had to walk to the middle of the orchard for privacy.

They squatted within a circle of trees and the oranges hung like big ornaments above their heads. The mother didn't consider it thievery when she plucked a few, so many were already rotting on the ground. The two were alone with no foreman to tell them the fruit they picked wasn't free, no one to stop her from giving Estrella an orange so big Estrella had to carry it to her father with two hands. Her father's boot rested on the insect-splattered bumper of their pickup. What impressed her most was the way his thumbnail plowed the peel off the orange in one long spiral, as if her father plowed the sun, as if it meant something to him to peel the orange from stem to navel without breaking the circle. Sometimes she remembered him with a mustache, sometimes smoking a Bugler tobacco cigarette, but always peeling an orange.

The women in the camps had advised the mother, *To run away from your husband would be a mistake.* He would stalk her and the children, not because he wanted them back, they proposed, but because it was a slap in the face, and he would swear over the seventh beer that he would find her and kill them all. Estrella's godmother said the same thing and more. *You'll be a forever alone woman*, she said to Estrella's mother, *nobody wants a woman with a bunch of orphans, nobody. You don't know what hunger is until your huercos tell you to your face, then what you gonna do?*

Instead, it was her father who'd ran away, gone to Mexico, the mother said at first, to bury an uncle just as they settled in a city apartment with the hope of never seeing another labor camp again. Estrella hadn't remembered a lot of those years, except that the twins started calling her mama. What she remembered most was the mother kneeling in prayer or the pacing, door slamming, locked bathroom, the mother rummaging through shoe boxes of papers, bills, addressed correspondence, documents, loose dollars hidden for occasions like this; the late-night calls, money sent for his return, screaming arguments long distance, bad connections, trouble at the border, more money sent, a sickness somewhere in between. Each call was connected by a longer silence, each request for money more painful. She remembered every job was not enough wage, every uncertainty rested on one certainty: food.

The phone was disconnected. She remembered the moving, all night packing with trash bags left behind, to a cheaper rent they couldn't afford, to Estrella's godmother's apartment, to some friends, finally to the labor camps again. Always leaving things behind that they couldn't fit, couldn't pack, couldn't take, like a trail of bread crumbs for her father. The mother didn't know about change-of-address cards or forwarding mail and for a while Estrella thought the absence of his letters was due to their own ignorance.

Estrella would never know of the father's repentance. Never know if he thought of them as the mother did of him. She could see it in the wet stone of the mother's eyes. —Is he eating an egg at this moment like I am eating an egg? Is he watching the moon like I am watching the moon, is he staring at a red car like I am, is he waiting like I am?

It didn't happen so fast, the realization that he was not coming back. Estrella didn't wake up one day knowing what she knew now. It came upon her as it did her mother. Like morning light, passing, the absence of night, just there, his not returning.

—You have no business in the barn, Perfecto wheezed in a voice like a whisper. His chest stretched as if his lungs were about to snap. The crying twins clung to Perfecto's belt, each pawing for his attention. He bent his head, clamped his hands on his knees to catch his breath and his hat tumbled onto the ground. The boys ran to the barn to hear him scold Estrella.

—Are you blind? Can't you see the walls are ready to collapse? You could've hurt the girls.

Perfecto sucked in air, his nostrils flaring. He wanted to say something else, but licked the dryness of his splintered lips instead.

—Go help your mother. Get going. NOW! Arnulfo and Ricky ran off laughing, but Estrella was stunned by the force of his words. Her chest breathed and crackled like kindling. Most of her braid had unraveled, and her loose long hair bent lazily around her chin. She flipped a few strands over her ear and stared at him and bit her lower lip. Finally, her cheeks as red as hot embers, Estrella stomped away. Perla picked up Perfecto's straw hat and handed it to him while Cookie wiped her runny nose with the back of her hand.

Estrella caught up with her brothers. She grabbed Ricky's striped green/brown T-shirt and shoved him forward, then jerked him back. He swung at the air with fists tight as walnuts. After a few jerks, she was satisfied with her revenge and let go. She heaved herself over the side board of the corral fence, flipped a leg and straddled it, then jumped down while her brothers ducked between two boards. Estrella led the way to the bungalow. Their heads bobbed over the shimmering of tall grasses.

15

—Ay come on, Star, Ricky called after her. Don't be mad.

—He's not my papa, Estrella said.

—So? asked Arnulfo, trying to keep up with her.

—Sew your pants, they're torn, she snapped, and she ran, her hair bouncing like a black tassel. Her brothers followed suit, and the twins scrambled after. Perfecto walked behind them all, fanning himself with his hat.

A car wreck waiting to happen, Petra had said. Estrella's real father looked up at her as he pulled out the old shoelaces. The freeway interchange right above their apartment looped like knots of asphalt and cement and the cars swerved into unexpected steep turns with squeals of braking tires. Sunlight glistened off the bending steel guardrails of the ramps. Just you wait and see, Petra said in a puff of breath on the window glass, a car will flip over the edge.

His new laces were too long and so he cut them with his single blade razor, the one he had brought with him all the way from Jerez, Zacatecas. He had pinched spit on the loose ends to rethread the laces carefully through the eyes of his shoe, then bent his chin to his knees as one foot vanished into a thick leathered shoe then the other. His back curved like a sickle against the window and her garlic-scented fingers ran up and down the beads of his spine. He was a man with lashes thick as pine needles, a man who never whispered; his words clanked like loose empty cans in a bag and she had to hush him in the presence of the sleeping children. Her fingers purred on his backbone until he stood up and walked out.

The traffic swelled and cars lined up on the curving on-ramp of the freeway until the cars yanked loose like a broken necklace and the beads scattered across the asphalt rolling, rolling, and she waited, her breath gone until the rubber treads of the tires connected with the pavement again.

He had the nerve, damn him, the spine to do it. She was almost jealous. The stories of his whereabouts stacked up like the bills she kept in a shoe box. Was it really him with a business in Ensenada selling bags of peanuts and ceramics? Was it him crossing Whittier Boulevard in Los Angeles with a woman who wore pumps so high she was almost as tall as him? Could it be? Petra lied to Estrella because she shouldn't know her father evicted all of them from the vacancy of his heart and so she lied right to her daughter's face, right through the cage of her very teeth and then she realized that truth was only a lesser degree of lies. Was it he who had the nerve to disappear as if his life belonged to no one but him?

She rolled the beads of the rosary between her fingers, made the sign of the cross, stopped his promises from flooding into her head and her mouth desperate, desperate for air. She was falling, toppling over a freeway bridge, her eyes shut to the swamp-colored trash bags squatting full of the family's belongings scattered about the room. Only noises hinted at another life: a neighbor dragged a trashcan out to the curb (morning); a toilet flushed (someone is home from work); the twins crying (mealtime); cars screeching with murderous brakes, long piercing dial tone of horns (the first of the month speeding faster than any car), the siren ring of the phone stilling her heart like spears of a broken clock.

Estrella had carried the fussing twins in the hoop of her arms, and sat them in front of an overturned zinc bucket and handed them wooden spoons. Petra could hear them right through the bathroom door. She had bitten the muscle of her thumb, tore flesh, then reeled herself back and ran cold water in the tub to vanish the blood drops like pomegranate seeds. The babies clanked the zinc bucket until the tin echos clamored and clinked like loud smashing car wrecks and Petra burst the door wide open. She clapped her hands against her ears and screamed Stop it, Stop it, Stop it! and the boys, terrified of her wailing, hid under the boxspring belly-ache down, until finally Estrella, with specks of green in her brown eyes, stood between her and the children, near the open cabinet where dead cockroaches brittled in the corner of the shelf and hollered You, *you* stop it, Mama! Stop this now!

Nothing in the cabinet except the thick smell of Raid and dead roaches and sprinkled salt on withered sun-flower contact paper and the box of Quaker Oats oat-meal. Estrella grabbed the chubby pink cheeks Quaker man, the red and white and blue cylinder package and shook it violently and its music was empty. The twins started to cry, and for a moment Estrella's eyes narrowed until Petra saw her headlock the Quaker man's paperboard head like a hollow drum and the twins sniffed their runny noses. One foot up, one foot down, her dress twirling like water loose in a drain, Estrella drummed the top of his low crown hat, slapped the round puffy man's double chins, beat his wavy long hair the silky color of creamy hot oats and the boys slid out from under the boxspring. Estrella danced like a loca around the room around the bulging bags around Petra and in and out of the kitchenette and up and down the boxspring, her loud hammering tomtom beats the only noise in the room.

Petra broke, her mouth a cut jagged line. She bolted out of the apartment, pounded down the plaster stairs through the parking lot and out into the street and ran some more. She stalled on the boulevard intersection divide and waited for the cars to stop, waited for him, for anyone, to guide her across the wide pavement; but the beads rolled on, fast howling shrieks of sharp silver pins just inches away from her.

Petra inspected her hands, remembering how their bodies were once like two fingers crisscrossing for good luck. Blood was crusting on the dots of her self-inflicted bite. The endless swift wind slapped against her face. The twins so hungry and her feet too heavy, too heavy to lift. Echos of voices, shouts of anger, threats of some

19

kind she could barely hear over the blasting horns. Then, she remembered her father who worked carrying sixty pounds of cement, the way he flung the sacks over his hunching shoulders for their daily meal, the weight bending his back like a mangled nail; and then she remembered her eldest daughter Estrella trying to feed the children with noise, pounding her feet drumming her hand and dancing loca to no music at all, dancing loca with the full of empty Quaker man. One foot up, one foot down, Petra finally pulled herself across the lanes of the wide fierce boulevard and car brakes screeched and bumpers crushed, and headlights exploded like furious tempers. One foot up, one foot down no more dancing with the full of empty Quaker man.

—You seen something? Alejo asked. The barn's ash shadow grew so long it humped over the corral fence and shimmied with the waves and tumble of the tall grasses. Alejo couldn't tell whether the figure was a dwarf adult or a stocky child who had slipped around the towering structure.

—I didn't see nobody.

—The kid might get hurt.

—We don't have time for this. ¿Entiendes Méndez? Gumecindo was unusually adamant. We're gonna do this or not?

—What's the hurry?

—The dark. That's the hurry.

—Looked like one of the García kids, Alejo said, and

he laid his bags of peaches against a tree and jogged toward the barn, trampling a path through the grasses. Gumecindo followed close behind. Their shadows brushed over etched initials which were carved in the wood siding: IBT, Joe H, a gouged heart, a few dates, letters joined by crosses, por vida. Rubble of tin and glass shards shined from the golden camouflage of straw near a side entrance, and except for the dried bird droppings which crunched like gravel under their shoes, the barn was silent.

—See? Nobody's around. Alejo felt Gumecindo's moist breath on his neck.

Alejo slowly rounded the corner. Between the eaves of the cedar shakes, stray swallows flew out from the straw and sprigs and featherdown. He pressed his belly against the loping wall carefully. A loose rusty nail snatched a buttonhole of his workshirt yanking him back. His shirt tore with a rip so loud they heard flutters coming from inside the rafters of the barn.

The cousins startled. Gumecindo nervously tilted his head straight up the wood sheeting until the sun glared like spokes of light that bore into his eyes and then the boy jumped out of nowhere, his short stumps of arms raised high, his face like a puff fish.

—See him? Right over there, Alejo said and pointed. Gumecindo blinked and water welled up in his eyes. Dust peppered their heads and Alejo hoped the boy would stay outside the barn. The skin of the boy's upper lip tugged up toward the beak of his nose and into

21

one of his flattened nostrils. He had never seen the boy before. Two black seeds glared at Alejo from the bubbled whites of his eyes, though they looked as if they were fixed on a space far above Alejo's head.

—This is too weird, 'mano, Gumecindo said. He rubbed an eye until it was pink-red and walked to where they had first laid their bags and leaned his back on the peach tree. Gumecindo shoved his hand deep in the back pocket of his dirty trousers and pulled out a paisley kerchief and wiped his eyes to clear his blurry vision.

The boy grew alert. Tossing shadows played on the mildewed trough and it struck Alejo as odd that the child was alone. The boy skittered about, playfully snapping his hands like loud castanets to catch the flitting shadows of the trees. Alejo felt relieved until the boy stumbled on some twigs and fell, and his elbow scraped against a broken glass. Alejo moved to comfort the boy, but the boy stepped back, his mouth a lopsided *O* as he held his bleeding elbow gingerly. It seemed to Alejo that he was crying, though all he heard were the wind-tossed trees. Even the gaping hole of his own shirt hung like a speechless mouth on his belly.

Alejo laid his fingers flat with his thumb beneath. He looped one finger up like a handle of a teacup and a swan appeared on the ground and eventually caught the boy's attention. The boy stared at the shadow swan gracefully swimming up and down the boundary of shade until it disappeared. Droplets of blood slowly trailed down the boy's wrist and he moved closer to the edge of shadow, as if it were a blanket he wanted to lift and search for the swan, when suddenly an elephant sprung from that very slab of gray, its trunk trumpeting in the air.

The boy was transfixed. He studied the elephant who metamorphosed into a long rabbit that hopped to and fro and then became a dog that jawed and yapped and sniffed the boy's elbow to his delight. But it was the eagle, majestic wingspan of fingers, that made the boy forget his injury, the eagle that fluttered from the tower of shade, gliding its wings into the sunlight. Sprinkling droplets of blood, the boy chased the bird as it wheeled above a discarded tire and rippled over some glass shards until it zigzagged across the dented trough and finally returned to the tower from where it first appeared, and vanished.

Not even a few drops of menstrual blood in his coffee would keep him from leaving. Estrella's father tore the last stick of gum in two, giving Petra one half. He unwrapped his piece and placed it in his mouth and chewed, tossing the tinsel wrapper onto the floor. Then he said he had to go and promised to return by the end of the week. But it was something Estrella said about his shoes with the new laces that made Petra realize he might not come back.

—Estrella, mi'ja, Petra had said, Papi's leaving. Say good-bye for now.

—Mama, hide his shoes so he won't go, Estrella pleaded. And it was too late, too late because the door slammed shut and Petra cupped the cry in her mouth, damming the pure white anger from spilling onto her daughter.

So what is this?

When Estrella first came upon Perfecto's red tool chest like a suitcase near the door, she became very angry. So what is this about? She had opened the tool chest and all that jumbled steel inside the box, the iron bars and things with handles, the funny-shaped objects, seemed as confusing and foreign as the alphabet she could not decipher. The tool chest stood guard by the door and she slammed the lid closed on the secret. For days she was silent with rage. The mother believed her a victim of the evil eye.

Estrella hated when things were kept from her. The teachers in the schools did the same, never giving her the information she wanted. Estrella would ask over and over, So what is this, and point to the diagonal lines written in chalk on the blackboard with a dirty fingernail. The script A's had the curlicue of a pry bar, a hammerhead split like a V. The small i's resembled nails. So tell me. But some of the teachers were more concerned about the dirt under her fingernails. They inspected her head for lice, parting her long hair with ice cream sticks. They scrubbed her fingers with a toothbrush until they were so sore she couldn't hold a pencil properly. They said good luck to her when the pisca was over, reserving the desks in the back of the classroom for the next batch of migrant children. Estrella often wondered what happened to all the things they boxed away in tool chests and kept to themselves.

She remembered how one teacher, Mrs. Horn, who had the face of a crumpled Kleenex and a nose like a hook—she did not imagine this—asked how come her mama never gave her a bath. Until then, it had never occurred to Estrella that she was dirty, that the wet towel wiped on her resistant face each morning, the vigorous brushing and tight braids her mother neatly weaved were not enough for Mrs. Horn. And for the first time, Estrella realized words could become as excruciating as rusted nails piercing the heels of her bare feet.

The curves and tails of the tools made no sense and the shapes were as foreign and meaningless to her as chalky lines on the blackboard. But Perfecto Flores was a man who came with his tool chest and stayed, a man who had no record of his own birth except for the year 1917 which appeared to him in a dream. He had a history that was unspoken, memories that only surfaced in nightmares. No one remembered knowing him before his arrival, but everyone used his name to describe a job well done.

He opened up the tool chest, as if bartering for her voice, lifted a chisel and hammer; aquí, pegarle aquí, to take the hinge pins out of the hinge joints when you want to remove a door, start with the lowest hinge, tap the pin here, from the top, tap upwards. When there's too many layers of paint on the hinges, tap straight in with the screwdriver at the base, here, where the pins widen. If that doesn't work, because your manitas aren't strong yet, fasten the vise pliers, these, then twist the pliers with your hammer.

Perfecto Flores taught her the names that went with the tools: a claw hammer, he said with authority, miming its function; screwdrivers, see, holding up various heads and pointing to them; crescent wrenches, looped pliers like scissors for cutting chicken or barbed wire; old wood saw, new hacksaw, a sledgehammer, pry bar, chisel, axe, names that gave meaning to the tools. Tools to build, bury, tear down, rearrange and repair, a box of reasons his hands took pride in. She lifted the pry bar in her hand, felt the coolness of iron and power of function, weighed the significance it awarded her, and soon she came to understand how essential it was to know these things. That was when she began to read.

Perfecto called from inside the bungalow, wanted her to open his tool chest and bring him thinner nails, the ones in the baby-food jar. The thicker nails splintered the brittle wood in two.

He kneeled and plugged a hole the size of a hand where the field mice came and went, and he placed the slivers of silver nails between his dry lips. His hair curved around his ears and fell straight back upon his neck in slick little waves and whenever he did not wear his hat, and the sun hit just so on his silver hair, it had a hint of tarnish. But he wore his hat mostly and his hat quivered as he hammered. The hammering was rhythmic, slow. It took three swings from the heavy ball of the hammer to secure each nail on the warped wood. He worked in a square of dusk from the window, and she saw his wide hand spread on the floor, a purple thumbnail. Perfecto leaned back, and pushed his bifocals up to inspect his repair.

—I'm not your papa. But you're getting me old with your . . .

—Where did you put the lantern?

—Stay away from the barn, hear me?

—You're right. You're not my papa.

—That should do it.

Although reluctant at first, Estrella helped him up from his knees by cupping her hand under his elbow. The room was now clean and safe to spread the blankets. They held a sky-blue sheet between them to divide the rooms. He held one corner, she another, and he nailed one corner, passed the hammer to her, and she did the other. He hammered a thick nail near the entrance and plucked off his hat and hung it. He then placed a bucket in the corner for the weak bladders of the twins who refused to go outdoors in the night.

—It will be good to sleep lying down, he said, dragging his feet outside.

—Where did you put the lantern? she asked again, following close behind.

Perfecto Flores was not her papa. In the last labor camp, near the water spigot where the farmworkers got their drinking water, Estrella used her knuckles to rip Maxine Devridge's mouth into a torn pocket to prove it.

There were ten Devridges in all, not counting the ones in prison, and the other families pitched tents as far away from them as possible. Of all the people who migrated to the fields, Maxine was the only one Estrella knew by last name. Last names were plentiful and easily forgotten because they changed with the crops and the seasons and state lines. But everyone remembered a Devridge. The mother warned Estrella to keep her distance. A head shorter and two years younger than Maxine, Estrella tried to ignore her even as she worked close enough to hear Maxine blurt out Kingdom Come or Christ Almighty whenever the sun was too hot or the drinking water ran out. By mid-harvest, with only a quarter of the tomato field picked, one of the Devridge boys, the one as skinny as a weed, was handcuffed and guided by the elbow across the camp yard to a four-door Buick Wildcat parked near the water pipe. The weed boy had such high regard for himself, the man with a ten-gallon hat had to push his head to his chin to get him in the car.

—Low life! Dumb frog, Maxine yelled and Estrella didn't know if she meant her own brother, the man, or Big Mac the Foreman, who waved the gawkers away. Maxine sat on her porch under the crooked awning of the Devridge wooden shack and gathered her printed dress above her knees, vising it between her legs. She watched the Buick drive away. A lumpy mattress leaned to one side of the house. She fanned herself with a magazine.

—Hey, you. Looky what I got, Maxine yelled, and she held the magazine up. Estrella cupped water and twisted the spigot off, and sucked the water from the palm of her hand. When she heard Maxine Devridge call, she brushed her wet fingers on her chest.

—Yeah, you. You talk 'merican? Maxine asked and Estrella glanced around to make sure the mother was not watching. The waistline of her dress ripped wider every time Estrella poked her fingers to scratch a patch of mosquito bites and she kept her fingers scratching as she walked toward the porch steps.

The blue stripes on the mattress had yellow teabag stains. The mother was disgusted at how the Devridges had no shame sun-drying the peed mattress in full view every morning. But if Maxine felt shameful of her brother's thievery or the peed mattress or the way her dress was hiked up between her legs, she didn't show it and she continued waving the magazine proudly.

Estrella stared at Maxine's red burnt cheeks. Her hair was so white on her face, her eyebrows were invisible. The glossy page of the magazine shone in the sun.

—You deaf, girl? Looky here, ain't this purty? and Maxine pointed to the picture of *Millie the Model*, her bold yellow hair in a flowing flip, her painted breasts perfect smiles on her chest. The model was crying, big tears melting from her ice blue eyes.

—I ain't got no cooties, stupid.

—Don't call me that.

—What they call you then?

—Star.

—Christ Almighty. What kinda name . . . like movie star? Maxine narrowed one inquiring eye and her hair, thin and stringy, laid flat on her round head. Orange peelings, cracked and chewed sunflower seeds were scattered around the porch steps. A dirty mason jar squatted on the railing with a trace of water in it.

—Why's she bawling?

—I dunno.

—Suit yourself. Maxine got up and the porch plank creaked. The dress she wore had a faded print of yellow corncobs with kernels falling and the corn kernels tumbled to her ankles. Standing on the step, she seemed taller and skinnier than her brother.

—Okay, okay. Gimme it. And Estrella grabbed the gloss in her hands. The teachers in the schools had never let her take picture books outside of the classroom. The only book she had ever owned was a catechism chapbook that her godmother had given her. Estrella had read and reread the chapbook I Believe in God *and The Holy Spirit came in the form of tongues of fire to show His love, and in a great wind to show the power of His grace.*

Maxine's book was light and Estrella flipped the first page open. The pictures had bubbles with words. Words like the kind in the newspapers thrown in trash cans at filling stations, or oatmeal instructions, or billboard signs that Estrella read over and over: *Clorox makes linens more than white. . . . It makes them sanitary, too! Swanson's TV Dinners, closest to Mom's Cooking. Coppertone—Fastest Tan Under the Sun with Maximum Sunburn Protection.* She traced her finger under the sentence of the first box of the comic.

—Read it out, Maxine said, turning to the fields beyond the water pipe and rows of labor shacks and beyond that to the tarps that fluttered like bats. She stood as straight as the ARGO woman on a box of corn starch. Then she looked down at her bare feet. She wriggled her yellow toes on the planks.

—I got a whole lot of other ones if you read me them. Maxine owned what her brothers stole, and what she owned was a crate of comic books.

—She likes him, Estrella explained and she pointed to a man with a camera around his neck.

—Figured it had to be over some man. Maxine sat on the porch again and her dress billowed and scattered

31

corn kernels upon her feet. She flapped the dress between her knees to make space for Estrella to sit.

—Tell it to me, she asked, and Estrella did and that was how it began.

Day after day, when the last row of tomatoes had been picked and the sun was low, Estrella walked down the road to meet Maxine, who waited with a scrolled-up comic book. She dragged her shoes across the softened soil, her back like boiled muscle, her water jug empty and smudged with her fingerprints. The fragrance of tomatoes lingered on her fingers, her hair, her pillow, into the next morning and throughout the day, until it became a thick smell that no longer simply lingered but stuck in her nose like paste.

Estrella would wave to Maxine and Maxine would wave back, leaning on one of the oaks, the scrolled-up comic vised under her arm while she unfastened her wrist cuff fold to up a sleeve. Estrella would walk toward her, a pair of trousers under her dress and an oversized, unbuttoned, long-sleeved shirt which would fly open and bend around her body.

They headed for the irrigation ditch and halted near the walk bridge. By then their throats were dry and sore and swallowing meant a painful raking. Estrella had heard through the grapevine about the water, and knew Big Mac the Foreman lied about the pesticides not spilling into the ditch; but the water seemed clear and cool and irresistible on such a hot day.

—Wanna go for a dip? asked Maxine, unstrapping her laces, but Estrella shook her head NO.

—You think 'cause of the water our babies are gonna come out with no mouth or something? Estrella asked, pushing up her sleeves. She lay on her stomach and dipped her bandanna into the water. The cool water ran over her fingers and over the gravel like velvet.

—Looky you. Thinkin' about babies 'ready, Maxine said, retying her shoe. All I know is that my ma's been drinking this water for forty some-odd years, and if you askin' me, she has too many mouths to feed. Maxine bent over the weeds and washed her face, moistened her lips, but this time neither of them took a drink.

Estrella and Maxine lay side by side in the cattail reeds near the ditch to read Maxine's favorite copy of *Millie the Model.* Maxine was in love with Clicker, the photographer, but wouldn't admit it and Estrella teased her about the sissy white boy. Maxine told her to shut her trap and squeezed closer for a better look at the soiled comic book. They were about to find the red-haired Sheila trying to seduce Clicker when the air became thick with the smell of rotting flesh.

—You break wind? asked Maxine, and Estrella laughed. Maxine stood and pointed. Looky, Looky, she said, along with a whole sentence of excited English words that didn't sound English at all to Estrella, Looky there! She pointed to a drowned, bloated dog, which floated down the canal. The carcass rolled on its back, its belly swollen and damp dark, then rolled back to its side, its legs like spears dipping gently toward the bridge until it passed them. The girls pinched their noses.

—Poor little dog, Estrella said. The stinking carcass stalled at a grate under the bridge. As soon as the carcass rested, a thick coat of horseflies appeared from nowhere. Estrella picked up a rock and pelted it. Maxine joined in her efforts to dislodge the carcass and make it go to the other side of the bridge. But the carcass did not move. The smell and flies too foul to withstand, they headed back to the camp. Maxine carried the scrolled-up comic book in her fist.

It was Maxine who started it, who liked to make words out of the silence of the long field they crossed and she rattled on like a broken wheel on a shopping cart until they reached the water pipe in the center of the labor camp. There they saw Perfecto Flores driving off to pick up the mother.

—Why your papa so old? Maxine asked.

—He's not my papa.

—Then why you let your grandpa fuck your ma fo'?

Estrella stopped. She halted Maxine with a jerk of her arm.

—What?

—Just weird, you know. My ma says it makes for one-legged babies not the wa . . .

—She isn't fucking him.

—And how'd you know that?

—'Cause he's not my papa.

—Jesus Henry Christ! Maxine replied incredulously. She began to laugh, her giggles bubbling like welling water when the irrigation pipe was twisted on. Sweet toast, don't you know nothin'?

—Shut your trap!

—They ain't dry-humping.

Estrella pulled Maxine's stringy sandy hair with such pure hatred it startled even her. For a moment she felt as if she could kill the white girl. She clawed and wrapped Maxine's hair around her fingers, pulling clump after clump. Maxine yelled and swung the scrolled comic book wildly at Estrella. Finally, they locked so tightly, so concentrated were their efforts to hurt one another, they fell silent, each grasping the other's hair with clawed fingers, their workshoes crushing and tearing the pages of the comic book under them. The boys ran from the tire swings, jumped the wooden fences, and circled the two girls wrestling each other to the ground. They hooted and catcalled. By the time Mrs. Devridge came running to whack a broom across Estrella's back, her shirt was in shreds, and the welts of her nipples showed naked. The boys pointed and laughed.

—You all go on home now 'fore I kill you myself, Mama Devridge said to Estrella, her wide chest heaving from the run. She had been eating a piece of bread, and swallowed the last of it.

—Go on now, you all. The boys jumped back, feeling the wind of the swinging broom.

Estrella stared at Maxine, waiting for her to say something like *forget it*, or *let's go look for the dead dog*, or *read me this one* or even, *what you do that fo'?* But Maxine's face was red and bloated, her upper lip thickening and she wiped her nose with the sleeve of her shirt. Maxine turned and Mama Devridge shoved her forward to their shack.

Estrella's tears stung her scratchy cheeks. She watched Mama Devridge's back hovering over Maxine. The boys circled her one last time, then left, bored at her stillness. Estrella stood. A young girl came and filled a bucket of water cautiously, then hurried away, half the water spilling against her leg. Estrella picked up the remains of the comic book and dusted it. The pages fell loose.

When Perfecto returned with the mother, Estrella would have to tell her about the fight and the mother would sit outside the tarpaulin tent with aching varicose veins and wait for Big Mac to drive up and tell them to move on for their own good on account of he wasn't responsible for harm or bodily affliction caused by the devil-sucking vengeful Devridges. Migrant families are tight, he would say, you ought to know. They look out for their own.

Perfecto would listen, his face like wrinkled khaki as he removed his bifocals and wiped them with the tail of his workshirt. He would not ask Estrella what the fight was about. He would think she is nothing but trouble, this big-legged girl with claws. He would open his tool chest, and ask her to loosen the mushroom spikes from the ground with a ball hammer, drag the agave hemp ropes around her elbow and hitching thumb in neat oval circles to avoid tangles. The twins would look for their shoes lost in a pile of clothes. The mother would remove the hands of Jesucristo and wrap them in socks and then wrap her statues in flour sack cloth and place them atop the dishes and pans in the zinc basin, after which, the mother would roll the doily scarf and place it in the glove compartment with the envelope of documents. Estrella would unscrew the corner pipes with two clamp wrenches. The boys would hide behind the trees, pick whatever was being harvested and return with pillowcases bulging. Then they would fill the plastic water bottles at the pipe. One of the twins would cry because a shoe was missing and nowhere to be found and did anybody see the dolly?

Perfecto would lay the long pipes on the flattened tarp, neatly roll them, dragging the tarp against the sun baked earth, and erasing the ruts of their shoeprints and the tracks of their boxes and Estrella would not care how angry he became for not being able to collect on a few days of work. And as they always did, sooner this time than later, they would leave, the comic book laying where her tracks had once been, its pages fluttering under a rock.

The wagon would pass the long rows of tomato

plants where the two girls had plucked tomatoes, rubbing off the white coating of insect spray with their shirt sleeves, and bitten into the hard greenish flesh with relish, adding salt and sucking the warm juicy seeds. The wagon would pass the massive oak tree which they climbed to reread *Millie the Model* on a lazy Sunday when they were supposed to be in church; passed the ditch where they saw the drowned dog. No one except Estrella saw Maxine follow the trail of dust left behind from the car. The two friends stared at each other until there was enough highway between them to bury their faces.

—¡'Mano, pronto! Gumecindo whispered, looking up at the soles of his cousin's shoes. They would be fired if they were caught, and Gumecindo wanted nothing more than for the strange day to end. But Alejo risked climbing onto a thinner and weaker branch to see farther down the canal of cool water. The girl squatted by the edge of the irrigation ditch, and cupped water to clean the mud off a watermelon. He saw her when they were about to call it quits for the night. The watermelon slipped from her hand and gently bobbed to the middle of the ditch, softly tumbling downstream.

Alejo held on to the peach. Tonight the two cousins had managed fifteen sacks of peaches though Gumecindo complained about every minute they spent in the orchard. They would sell the peaches at the flea market on Sunday, and Alejo knew his griping cousin would pat the outline of the bulging billfold in his pocket contentedly. Alejo watched her follow the watermelon downstream until it was close enough to the edge and she could reach for it. But it slipped and bobbed idly away.

—Almost, Alejo whispered.

—You seeing things again?

Alejo knew Gumecindo found the dark and the screaming hours before frightening. His cousin had not stopped talking of La Llorona and the ghosts of her drowned children, and Alejo was forced to hear the stories with every tree he climbed. No, Gumecindo wanted him to hurry not because of the Foreman or loss of employment. La Llorona was more threatening.

—There's a girl over there, Alejo whispered.

—It's the sun, 'mano. Fried your sesos.

Alejo could barely make her out before the twilight turned her into a silhouette. She hadn't even looked around.

—Pronto, 'mano. Estoy pensando en garrapatas, no garranalgas.

—Ssssh.

—I'm hungry.

It was probably not as smooth as he imagined and it took less than a minute, the way she gathered her printed dress up and over her bare buttocks, to the small of her back, over her neck, and onto the weeds.

—You're cooking tonight, Gumecindo said, and he promised himself he would work scrubbing the Hamburger King floor with a toothbrush before accepting another fruit-picking job again.

She sliced through the cool irrigation water, opening her legs like a frog to propel herself to the watermelon, the bulbs of her buttocks bobbing. The water was quiet and licked around her in velvet waves as the moonlight broke like chipped silver. It was then that Alejo lost his footing. The branch gave way under his weight and cracked and he slipped through the foliage in a rustle. For a moment, Gumecindo didn't know what hit him.

Te vengo a decir adiós, No quiero verte llorando. Petra whispered the lyrics under her breath as she poked the dying cinders of the fire, and the ash collapsed upon itself. *Estoy viendo tus ojitos que de agua se están llenando.* In the waning cast of embers, she watched her daughter come forth from the well of darkness where the lines of eucalyptus trees intersected. Estrella cradled a watermelon like a baby and this vision saddened her. Petra bent to scratch a mosquito bite swelling. She wanted her children to stay innocent and honest, wanted them to be as content as when they first arrived somewhere; but she forced them to be older for their own safety. The song lingered like the taste of vanilla on her tongue. Petra watched her daughter growing right before her eyes.

—Tu espalda está toda mojada, she said.

Estrella's long hair clung to the sides of her face, wetness dampening the back of her dress. At first Estrella thought the mother had been waiting for her. Instead, when she eclipsed the glow of light from the fire to place the watermelon on the table, she realized her mother's stare went off to the road. It was only then that Estrella noticed the missing wagon.

—Where's Perfecto? she asked, and bundled her black hair up. Though the winds had died down, the dampness of her dress was giving her chills and she gave her back to the warmth of the dying fire.

—Gone to the ranch store to start some credit, the mother replied. Estrella drummed the melon so that the slapping sound distracted her.

—If Perfecto doesn't come, we can eat the melon in the morning, Estrella said. She headed for the room where the children slept, where she would snuggle between the warm bodies of the twins.

—He'll be back, the mother replied.

—Come to bed, Mama.

—*Yo no quisiera separarme de tu lado* . . . She poked the fire. Estrella?

—Yeah, Mama?

—Perfecto killed a niño de tierra. She raised the stick in the direction of the porch. It was still warm from her grasp.

—Aquí? Estrella asked, staking the soil right in front of the porch and the mother nodded and Estrella guided the stick and began the demarcation around the house while the mother sang softly. She grated the stick against the rocky soil, dragging the stick to the side and then to the back of the house where the verses of the song were lost in the chorus of crickets until she returned to the point from where she first began then retraced the line again for a deeper, more definite oval. The mother believed scorpions instinctively scurried away from lines which had no opening or closing. Estrella never questioned whether this was true or not. She handed the stick back to the mother.

—Come inside, Mama.

—In a minute.

—Don't you ever get tired? Estrella asked.

—And? The mother turned to study the daughter, then returned to her accustomed vigil. *Ojalá Diós lo permita, Pa' estrecharte entre mis brazos, Pa' estrecharte entre mis brazos.*

Alejo trampled through the soft soil of the peach orchard with quick, sure steps. By the time he reached the long line of eucalyptus trees, the morning fog had dissipated and he could see a coil of smoke rising not much farther down the road. He put down the sack he carried and rested, and he took in the scent of seawater salt and burning wood and damp air. Between the rows of trees, Alejo caught sight of the biplane. A few miles east a white biplane zipped over the acres of grapes. Its buzzsaw motor descended, low, straight. The plane dusted the crops with long efficient sprays of white cloudy chemicals, then ascended to dust another row

42

farther away on the horizon. The birds, with their blank and nervous eyes, began to caw.

Ricky called Arnulfo to come see the biplane. He stood at the window of the bungalow and pointed out the plane to his brother, his hair stuck straight up from a full night of sleep. In the distance they could see it over the treeline of tall eucalyptus. Ricky motioned with his hand its smooth turn and whispered to Arnulfo, because the twins were still asleep, that he wanted to be a pilot and fly a biplane just like that one. Arnulfo yawned, tasted his sleep, then returned to a bundle of blankets that made up his bed.

Alejo lifted the sack and flipped it over his shoulder. His high-top tennis shoes disturbed the leafhoppers who jumped out of the way and his shoes snapped the twigs and molten leaves and a few birds flew out from under the fallen branches of the eucalyptus. Their wings spread then glided over Estrella as she gripped the handle of the blackened bucket she was removing from the fire. The handle was wrapped in rags, and her face glowed warm from the steaming water. The other bucket of boiled water was cooling for the day's drinking. She dipped an enamel cup, and drank the lukewarm water. She stared over the lip of the cup at Alejo approaching, carrying a bulky sack.

He wore black shoes that stuck way out in front of him. She noticed right away how big his feet were. He was bigger than his trousers and the cuffs rode high above his ankles. He walked over to the mother, her sweater sleeves pulled up, a steel pot between her knees, intent on cleaning the pinto beans, picking out the pebbles with an experienced eye.

—Buenas, cómo 'stan? His voice was not manly, like her father's, or authoritative like Perfecto's, nor did his voice sound like the other men who sat around a bonfire on a Saturday night, passing a bottle and talking about home and the loves left behind. He rubbed his throat. The kindling snapped in the pit where coffee boiled. Smoke, cold, garlic and coffee smelled.

Estrella cracked some twigs in two, stuck a few in the fire. It looked like he swallowed something that stuck in his throat. It looked like he had swallowed a stone.

—My name's Alejo y estoy muy lejos de donde nací. Como la canción Mixteca, he joked. He placed the sack of peaches on the makeshift table for the mother to accept. For you, he said, Please take them, and the mother smiled, shook and emptied its contents. The lush peaches thumped on the wooden table, one rolling off the edge until Estrella broke its fall. As Estrella weighed it with the palm of her hand, Alejo stood nervously, his fingers in his pockets, his thumbs sticking out.

—We got here right before the store closed, said the mother. In the empty sack, the mother poured six tin cups of pinto beans from a ten-pound sack that Perfecto had managed to get out of the store owner after snaking

44

the man's backroom toilet until it flushed. She rolled a few flour tortillas in half, added them to the contents of the sack.

—Llévalos a tu Mamá, she said, from us.

—My mother's dead, and Alejo cleared his voice, but the stone of his throat did not go away, My grandma's in Texas. Then he added, I'm here with a cousin, saying it because he thought for a moment she would take the beans back as if not having a mother meant he had no family. He held the bag like a noose.

—They brought us on a bus, me and Gumecindo and the others, Alejo continued, and his words jumped and bumped into each other and he felt his face grow hot. Estrella flipped her long black hair to the side, and bit the peach with a deep ravenous bite.

—Don't let them see you take the fruit, Estrella warned, licking a finger that dripped with sweet juice. The skin between her thick eyebrows gathered into a thunderbolt when she bit again.

—For the pay we get, they're lucky we don't burn the orchards down. This came from the mother.

—No sense talking tough unless you do it, replied Estrella, which gave Alejo the idea that this is the way they always talked with one another. Estrella held up the fruit close to the mother's mouth.

—Great peach, Mama, and the mother bit into the meat of the peach, raised her eyebrows in surprise, and nodded in agreement.

Ricky dove from the porch, his arms extended and

circled the table, then swooped down with one quick precise move and clawed a peach like a hawk would a rodent.

—Star can't get me, Star can't get me, Ricky chanted.

—You wish, Estrella replied, and sucked the wooden pit.

He thanked them again most graciously and walked until he was out of sight and then he turned back to see the coils of smoke. Alejo did not really see Estrella's face, her pierced but bare earlobes which were long and oval. Did not see the deep pock scar above her eyebrow from a bout of measles or the way her eyes had green specks like her father's. What he saw was the woman who swam in the magnetic presence of the full moon, a woman named Star.

Two

*T*he white light of the sun worked hard. Even the birds wavered on the crest of the heat waves. Under the leafy grapevines, the grapes hung heavy. She had readied the large rectangular sheet of newsprint paper over an even bed of tractor levelled soil, then placed the wooden frame to hold the paper down. Now, her basket beneath the bunches, Estrella pulled the vine, slit the crescent moon knife across the stem, and the cluster of grapes was guided to the basket below.

Carrying the full basket to the paper was not like the picture on the red raisin boxes Estrella saw in the markets, not like the woman wearing a fluffy bonnet, holding out the grapes with her smiling, ruby lips, the sun a flat orange behind her. The sun was white and it made

Estrella's eyes sting like an onion, and the baskets of grapes resisted her muscles, pulling their magnetic weight back to the earth. The woman with the red bonnet did not know this. Her knees did not sink in the hot white soil, and she did not know how to pour the baskets of grapes inside the frame gently and spread the bunches evenly on top of the newsprint paper. She did not remove the frame, straighten her creaking knees, the bend of her back, set down another sheet of newsprint paper, reset the frame, then return to the pisca again with the empty basket, row after row, sun after sun. The woman's bonnet would be as useless as Estrella's own straw hat under a white sun so mighty, it toasted the green grapes to black raisins.

Alejo snipped his own flesh and dropped his knife. He pressed the wound between his lips, tasted mud and salt and tin and then heard a lost child's wailing over the hundreds of rows. The vast field of grapevines was monotonous—without beginning, without ending—always the same to the piscadores and then to their children. Another child had wandered off and he could hear the scolding of a mother who was so relieved to find her daughter, she was angry.

Alejo thought of his own grandmother working in Edinburg, Texas, ironing, babysitting, cleaning houses, cutting cucumbers with lemon, salt, and powdered chile to sell at the Swap Meets, or making tamarind and hibiscus juices to sell after Sunday mass. She would do anything to allow her grandson to get schooling. Right this minute, as he pressed his lips to his wound, he imagined his grandma walking down Chávez Street, cutting across the park to get to the bus stop. Alejo readjusted his L.A. Dodger cap and tried to set the wooden frame with one hand. The other, with its torn skin, seemed painfully useless.

Estrella was not more than four when she first accompanied the mother to the fields. She remembered crying just as the small girl was wailing now. The mother showed pregnant and wore large man's pants with the zipper down and a shirt to cover her drumtight belly. Even then, the mother seemed old to Estrella. Yet, she hauled pounds and pounds of cotton by the pull of her back, plucking with two swift hands, stuffing the cloudy bolls into her burlap sack, the row of plants between her legs. The sack slowly grew larger and heavier like the swelling child within her.

Today was Alejo's turn to bring the lunch. He had packed burritos made of fried potato and French's mustard wrapped in flour tortillas, with fresh jalapeños crunchy like apples, that he and Gumecindo ate quietly under the shade of the grapevines. His Dodger cap rested on his knee.

Estrella sat under a vine. The sun shone through, making the leaves translucent. She could see their bones. And she could see the inside of her water bottle when she held it up to measure its contents. The water was tepid with particles floating like pieces of exploded stars in space and she drank in deep gulps, long and hard.

Alejo struggled with a piece of newsprint paper. His grandmother had reassured him, this field work was not forever. And every time he awoke to the pisca, he thought only of his last day here and his first day in high school. He planned to buy a canvas backpack to carry his books, a pencil sharpener, and Bobcat book-covers; and planned to major in geology after gradu-ating. He loved stones and the history of stones because he believed himself to be a solid mass of boulder thrust out of the earth and not some particle lost in infinite and cosmic space. With a simple touch of a hand and a hungry wonder of his connection to it all, he not only became a part of the earth's history, but would exist as the boulders did, for eternity.

Estrella remembered the mother trying to keep her awake, but the days were so hot, and the sun wanted her to sleep so badly, she became cranky and angry. Finally, the mother gave in, laid a four-year-old Estrella right on top of her bag of cotton, hushing her to sleep and Estrella never realized the added weight she must have been on the mother's shoulders as she dragged the bag slowly between the rows of cotton plants. At least this was how she remembered it: being lulled to sleep by the softness of the cotton, palms pressed together under her cheek, and the mother's pull almost gentle and pleasing, remembered how good it felt to close her eyes, to rest, to be this close to the mother's pull.

A young boy of ten hobbled onto Alejo's row. It was the same boy, he recalled, who mimicked the hawk a few days before. Alejo greeted him with a wave of his cap, but the boy continued walking, punching holes in the soft soil with his steps, barely lifting a hand to return the greeting.

Ricky found Estrella's row. He looked feverish and she put down her basket of grapes and pressed the water bottle to his lips, tilted it to the sky, asked him *where is your hat and where are Arnulfo and Perfecto Flores anyways? No sense walking home when the sun is the meanest. You don't know how to work with the sun yet,* she told him and she set him down under the vines. *Sit until you hear the trucks honking, go that way, okay?* Estrella turned and pointed, but her eyes fell on the flatbeds of grapes she had lined carefully, sheet after sheet of grapes down as far as she could see. Her tracks led to where she stood now. Morning, noon, or night, four or fourteen or forty it was all the same. She stepped forward, her body never knowing how tired it was until she moved once again. Don't cry.

Estrella carried the full basket with the help of a sore hip and kneeled before the clusters of grapes. The muscles of her back coiled like barbed wire and clawed against whatever movement she made. She closed her eyes and pulled in the memory of the cool barn, its hard-packed clay floor where she had gathered straw to sit, her knees to her chin. The swallows ticked their claws against the slope of the roof, the breeze wheezing between the planks like wind blowing over the mouth of a crater. All the day's clamped heat, all the cramping of her worked muscles would ease and hum above her like the music of a windpipe and she opened her eyes and spread the grapes and did not cry.

Alejo's grandmother had reassured him; he came from a long line of intelligent people, not like his cabeza de burro father, God rest his stupid soul; seize the chance and make something of yourself in this great and true country. He imagined her at the market by now, carting a few discarded *Reader's Digest*s for him to read, fingering the crookneck squash or maroon yam she would roast in foil on top of the comal and eat with a little margarine for dinner while sipping her daily cup of hot pinole or the cornsilk tea she said was good for her kidneys. His grandmother's hands turned cold at night and if he were home, he would be rubbing them with camphor balsam as thick as vaseline right this minute, then wrapping them with a towel warmed in the oven. He took her words seriously and wanted to do what was needed to continue the line and tried not to think of tomorrow. Alejo hoped she had received his money order.

The piscadores heard the bells of the railroad crossing somewhere in the distance and they stopped to listen. The trabajadores like Señora Josefina who might be thinking about what to make for dinner; Ricky, his arms clasped over his stomach, thinking of a Blue Bell ice cream sandwich, artificially flavored; or Gumecindo who might be planning his Saturday night. Piscadores like Florente of the islands who might be pinching his nostrils to blow his nose; Perfecto Flores who might be thinking how hard this work is for such an old man; the children who might be pulling and tugging the rope tied to the waists of their weary mamas so they wouldn't get lost; Arnulfo who might be afraid of the snakes that loved to jump out at him by surprise; Alejo who might be searching beyond the vines, and Estrella who might be kneeling over the grapes with her eyes closed—all of them stopped to listen to the freight train rattling along the tracks swiftly, its horn sounding like the pressing of an accordion. The lone train broke the sun and silence with its growing thunderous roar and the train reminded the piscadores of destinations, of arrivals and departures, of home and not of home. For they did stop and listen.

Alejo placed the frame atop the sheet of paper haphazardly. He flattened a few vine leaves to watch the freight cars race past him in the distance. Only after the train disappeared did he see Estrella wiping the sweat from the inside of her straw hat with a bandanna. She retied the bandanna across her nose and securely fastened it with large black bobby pins which weighed it down to protect her lungs on days like today when the fields were becoming dust-swept. All he could see was her bandanna fluttering with her moist breath. Alejo had been working right next to Estrella all along. How could he not have known?

Under his cap, a breeze raked wisps of hair which fell on his forehead and it felt so good on his face. He wanted her to notice him and figured if he hoped enough, she would. But all she did was continue her work, spreading the grapes evenly, then lifting the frame. His own paper slipped from under the slender frame and tossed and bounced away like old news down the long row of grapevines and he dashed forth to retrieve it.

For a moment, Estrella did not recognize her own shadow. It was hunched and spindly and grew longer on the grapes. Then she noticed another overshadowing her own, loitering larger and about to engulf her and she immediately straightened her knees and rubbed her eyes. She went over to the vine clutching her knife.

She saw a piscador running down the row, as if the person was being chased by something. The hot soil burned through her shoes as she made her way to the other side of the row. There she saw the bend of a back, and at first could not tell whether it was female or male, old or young, and Estrella called out. The back unfolded and it was Toothless Kawamoto. He pressed his hand on the small of his back and arched. Estrella sensed the awkwardness as he stood there uncertain as to why she called. Estrella thought quickly, and offered him the one peach she had saved to eat after work, a reward to herself. She held it up and he nodded and she tossed it to him, a long arc in the air, and he caught it with crooked fingers and placed it near his water jug with a smile so wide, his mouth looked like a vacant hole. He thanked Estrella, but it was she who was thankful.

The honking signaled the return of the trucks and the piscadores gathered their tools and jugs and aches and bags and children and pouches and emerged from the fields, a patch quilt of people charred by the sun: brittle women with bandannas over their noses, their salt-and-pepper hair dusted brown; young teens rinsing their faces and running wet fingers through their hair; children bored, tired, and antsy; and men so old they were thought to be dead when they slept. All emerged from the silence of the fields with sighs and mutters and, every now and then, laughter. A mother fingered a kerchief and poked the horns in her son's ear, while another teased the chin of her baby. The piscadores slapped themselves to chase away the dust of the day while children proudly hooked the necks of their fathers. A teenage girl playfully pounced on the shoulders of her boyfriend and laughed.

The Foreman produced a tablet of tables and columns of numbers, scribbled rows completed, names, erased calculations while the piscadores climbed the flatbed trucks. Gumecindo stood on top offering a hand to pull a piscador up. Alejo shoved his cap in his back pocket, fixed his hair in the side view mirror of the truck. He waited near the rear bumper to lift a child up by the waist to the outstretched arms of a mother.

Alejo sought Estrella. The trucks followed the railroad tracks which passed the orchards and fields, rumbled and rocked and jerked to a stop whenever someone knocked on the rear window. Before the last truck departed, Alejo's glance finally fell upon her. He watched her stooped body step on the ties of the railroad track as if she were cautiously climbing a ladder.

Estrella walked because of the playing field, her basket, jug, and knife bundled under the crook of her arm. She waved to the piscadores and the children waved to her from between the side panels of the trucks, then continued her walk along the tracks, almost regretful she had not taken the ride.

She reached the baseball diamond before dusk, the skies like whipped clouds with linings of ripe nectarine red. Estrella sat on the rail track, still hot from the day's sun, and hugged her knees to her chin. Two Little League teams played on the green of the lawn, behind the tall wire mesh fence. The players had just run out on the chalked boundaries. Parents and other spectators sat on lawn chairs behind the batter's bench or scattered about on the bleachers, ice chests at arm's reach. Estrella wished she had not surrendered her peach and thought how perfect the evening would be if she had the fruit to eat.

She squinted at the batter in his bleached white uniform going up to bat. Number Four. He seemed blurred in the mesh of fence. Her brother Arnulfo had talked about playing baseball. Ricky wanted to fly.

Another truck rolled past and she waved and they waved until she was alone on the tracks. The remaining sunlight clung to the clouds like a faint trace of lipstick. The sound of contact, of a ball splitting a bat, dull snap of wood, turned her attention to the game and the spectators cheered and she saw the ball suspended above left field and the players converged, their arms to the sky, the ball like a peach tossed out to hungry hands. The spectators rose and Estrella jumped to her feet to see mitts form holes like Mr. Kawamoto's mouth readied for the catch. One short player in a blue uniform took the ball out of the cradle of his glove and held it up as she had done with the peach and the audience broke out in sporadic applause.

Still on her feet, Estrella turned to the long stretch of railroad ties. They looked like the stitches of the mother's caesarean scar as far as her eyes could see. To the north lay the ties and to the south of her, the same, and in between she stood, not knowing where they ended or began.

Estrella gathered her knife and basket. She startled when the sheets of high-powered lights beamed on the playing field like headlights of cars, blinding her. The round, sharp white lights burned her eyes and she made a feeble attempt to shield them with an arm. The border patrol, she thought, and she tried to remember which side she was on and which side of the wire mesh she was safe in. The floodlights aimed at the phantoms in the field. Or were the lights directed at her? Could the spectators see her from where she stood? Where was home? A ball hit, a blunt instrument against a skull. A player ran the bases for the point. A score. Destination: home plate. Who would catch the peach, who was hungry enough to run the field in all that light? The perfect target. The lushest peach. The element of surprise. A stunned deer waiting for the bullet. A few of the spectators applauded. Estrella fisted her knife and ran, her shadow fading into the approaching night.

—¿Qué diablos te' ta pasando? asked the mother. She kneeled beside the zinc basin filled with water where the twins were squeezed in and taking a bath. Towels and calzones and trousers and T-shirts dried on a rope tied from a small tree to the pillar of the porch. A silver washboard lay on top the oak stump. Other shirts and pants clung onto the ground scrub surrounding the bungalow. The mother held a steel can full of water over Perla's head, then poured. ¿Por qué corres?

Estrella had run past the cooking pit, the table with its pots and pans and chipped dishes, jumped on the porch of their bungalow almost stumbling on a missed step. She dropped the empty water bottle and basket, and her pisca knife, and a piece of foil she saved to wrap tomorrow's lunch tumbled off the porch.

—Gonna teach someone a lesson.

—¿Qué dices? What?

She opened the tool chest, her breathing hard, and rummaged through Perfecto's tools until she found the thick pry bar.

—Put that away.

—Someone's trying to get me.

—It's La Migra. Everybody's feeling it, the mother explained. The twins began kicking each other over space and the fighting upset the mother more. Te voy a dar un nalgazo con la correa. She fished for Cookie's hand in the murky bath water to smack it, but smacked Perla's by mistake which caused a wail of injustice and more shoving.

The mother struggled upward, straightening one knee then the other, and Estrella noticed how purple and thick her veins were getting. Like vines choking the movement of her legs. Even the black straight skirt she wore seemed tighter and her belly spilled over the belt of waist, lax muscles of open births, her loose ponytail untidy after the laundry.

Today had been wash day. She had used the last of the ground yucca roots for soap and had to grind more stiff root which meant more work. Her knuckles were raw white against her coffee skin. The mother used the remaining rinse water to bathe the twins, although night approached.

—How you feeling today, Mama?

—Ya no hay ajo. And this was all she needed to say.

The mother ate five cloves of garlic pickled in vinegar every day to loosen her blood and ease her varicose veins; without the garlic, her veins throbbed.

—Maybe we can get some.

—What do you think? she replied. Her body seemed as faded in the dusk as the duck-print apron she wrung her hands in. She held a towel, hooked Cookie's armpit and Cookie resisted, slapping the water in protest, splashing the mother's face. Yo ya no voy a correr. No puedo más. With one clean sweep, she lifted Cookie out of the basin and walked to the table, her rubber slippers clicking.

—No sense telling La Migra you've lived here all your life, the mother continued as she dried her face with the towel. Cookie dripped like a soaked kitten on the table and whined about being cold and the mother dried her diligently, buffing her hair, her little birdbone chest, moved to her belly, apricot vagina, finally to her rubbery thighs and legs.

—Do we carry proof around like belly buttons?

—Something's out there, Estrella said.

—Ya cállate before you spook the kids.

—Where's Arnulfo? Ricky was sick today.

—Stop it.

—And Perfecto Flores?

—Con eso basta.

Estrella sat on the porch. She laid the crowbar across her lap, grasping it with two fists until her hands began to sweat. Her eyes hurt badly, and she wanted to close them but knew the mother would need help to make dinner. Perla stuck her toes out of the gray water and wriggled them.

—Don't run scared. You stay there and look them in the eye. Don't let them make you feel you did a crime for picking the vegetables they'll be eating for dinner. If they stop you, if they try to pull you into the green vans, you tell them the birth certificates are under the feet of Jesus, just tell them. The mother paused, still not turning around and Estrella could see the track of bra etched across her T-shirt back.

The mother raised her voice over Cookie's whining.

—Tell them que tienes una madre aquí. You are not an orphan, and she pointed a red finger to the earth, Aquí. The mother turned abruptly and fished Perla out next, and the twin began wailing. Estrella watched from the porch as the mother worked to dry Perla, this time jumpy, more concentrated. Cookie, her buttocks like shiny garbanzo beans, tan white against the brown of her skin, climbed down the table, and splashed back into the water.

Estrella closed her eyes, not wanting to open them again.

—¿Y tu primo? asked one of the piscadores. The group waited by the trees for the truck. One of the women pulled her long hair through the circle of a rubber band and her chestnut hair sheened against the bright sun. Some of the piscadores tied triangle bandannas around their heads anticipating the heat.

63

—Taking a leak, replied Gumecindo.

—¿Cómo? He seemed not to understand.

—A poco no sabes ai take a leak?

—Qué es eso, take un leak?

—¿En serio? Gumecindo mused.

—Regaron las plantas, replied a man whose lunch was tied to his waist in a pouch and carried the aroma of a wife's cooking.

—¿De dónde eres?

—Del Valle del Río Grande.

—¿Es un estado en México?

—Texas ya es parte de los Estados Unidos.

—Ay, said another, nodding his head as if he had known that Texas was a part of the United States all along. He tipped his water bottle and wet a kerchief, dabbing his face which was the color of worn leather and which made him look older than his thirty years.

—Sí lo sé, said another. Muy bonito. Muchas chicharras.

—¡Como música de maracas!

—Sí lo sé, Gumecindo sighed. He could almost hear the thick rattling of the cicadas in the trees which lined the park on Chávez Street back in Edinburg. As children, Alejo and he would cover their ears at the maraca noise. Gumecindo glanced around for his cousin. He had never thought it such beautiful music until this morning. The F700 diesel Ford truck bumped forward.

Alejo urinated behind the trees while the driver blasted the horn impatiently. He hurried to zip up but the steel teeth jammed and he saw two children peering from between the sideboards. They stared at him running toward the truck, one hand covering his half-closed zipper, the other holding onto his lunch. His baseball cap flipped off his head and he backtracked to retrieve it, his hands full, and the children covered their mouths in laughter. The driver went over to the back bumper and unhooked the door and someone offered a hand. Alejo and Gumecindo each grasped it in turn and heaved onto the truck. The driver closed the door, then slipped the iron bolt through the notch and returned to the front seat and the truck started with a jerk.

Ricky shoved Arnulfo, who shoved Estrella, who shoved Perfecto to make room for them to sit. Perfecto leaned near the rearview window, one arm over the truck bed while the other cradled his hat which sat on his lap like an expectant child. He scooted to one side without opening his eyes. Arnulfo's head lay on Estrella's lap and she ran her fingers through his hair gently and this reminded Alejo of sea froth reaching through the sand of a beach. She nodded hello, then tucked a few strands of loose hair over her ear. Only her mouth seemed visible under the shade of her straw hat.

Alejo could feel the steel of the zipper against him. He palmed his hair back, fingered his baseball cap, and Gumecindo elbowed him, pointing his chin and Alejo pulled himself away from his cousin's teasing. Her chest jiggled like flan custard beneath her shirt whenever the truck bounced.

—It's sure gonna be hot today, isn't it, Star? The other piscadores turned to Alejo then turned away. He tugged the flap of his baseball cap down, tried his voice over the noisy muffler.

—The lone star. Like the Texas flag. Estrella kept her glance over the sideboard and he vied for her attention again. It's such a pretty name, Star.

Finally he repeated it, his voice rising over the muffler and the black exhaust and the shouting startled her and this embarrassed him. Gumecindo rolled his eyes in disbelief. But her cheeks began to round slightly as her lips began to widen and Alejo's lips grew into a smile as well and Gumecindo looked away trying not to laugh.

—My papa was the one who named me that. She pinched Arnulfo's ear as she stroked his hair and he grunted a complaint. She glanced at Perfecto who slept soundly.

—What does he call you now?

—My papa's gone.

—Dead?

—Things just happen, she said, without conviction.

—What about him? And he pointed to Perfecto. When he heard Alejo's voice, Perfecto opened one eye under his bifocals, but did not flinch, then closed it once again for the remainder of the trip.

—Huh?

—What about him?

—I can't hear you.

—What things happen? he asked.

—I don't know. Things. She shrugged her shoulders and busied herself reading the faded washing instructions on the label of Arnulfo's T-shirt.

—How many brothers you got? Alejo asked. She bit her bottom lip as if she was thinking. He could barely see her almond eyes under the shade of a hat which was beginning to unravel at the rim.

—That's kinda a funny question.

—You don't like questions?

—Not really. Only asking maybe.

—What's your full name?

—Talk louder.

—Last name. What's your last name?

—What's it to you? she snapped back.

The truck slowed, then bumped cautiously along the railroad tracks. The piscadores bumped into one another like loose change in a pocket, until the truck crossed the tracks and continued its journey to the far end of the ranch. Arnulfo sat up and yawned and began to whimper, but Estrella gently drummed her fingers on his lips to hush him. The truck finally stopped, and everyone stretched and gathered up their muscles. The driver released the bolt of the back door, and the first of the piscadores were herded out of the corraled flatbed.

One hand in his trouser pocket, fingering a polished chip of obsidian stone, a few pennies. The other hand rounding a fat blue bottle of cola.

Estrella sat on top of the corral fence. She swung her legs, her untied shoelaces dangling like drawstrings. The chalk-white disc of the full moon shed light that slipped over the contours of the orchards, then over the roof of the distant barn, and reached the corral and finally lit the tips of her boots. Alejo stopped to the left of her, rounding the bottle, an elbow propped up on the corral board.

The other spectators, mostly men, waited by the fence. One of them whistled a long, mournful ballad while another tried remembering the lyrics of *Dos pasajes* or *Me voy pa'l norte*. A few drank warm bargain beer in aluminum cans then smashed the empties for recycling with a stomp of a shoe. Two children sat on a fallen tree trunk not far from the gate and laughed without looking up, cracking unsalted peanuts and hurling the shells into the weeds. Someone had set a bonfire down the deep end of the road like a beacon for them to find their way back to their beds and Alejo could see the sizzling red sparks spear up into the night.

Estrella waved away a whirl of gnats. *The Holy Spirit came in the form of tongues of fire to show His love* . . . and the words seemed to come alive because she saw nips of flames flick like tongues lapping the dark away. The owls hooted and every once in a while one of the men slapped a mosquito away or someone laughed hard enough to make her wonder about the joke. In front of her, one child rolled an abandoned tire to another, the wobbly tire often nicking her boots.

There was glazed light in her eyes he noticed, but turned to view the full moon turning into a coppery blare. Alejo passed the blue bottle and she took it silently and pressed the thick spout to her lips and drank and licked her lips. Her boots looked like corks, light and airy, and she returned the bottle and he drank, amber it seemed against the diminishing light of the moon.

His slicked back hair smelled thick with Brillecream. He tilted his head back into a long and graceful line, and the stone of his throat moved when he gulped. She recalled the curvature of the bottle in her hand, the velvet cool and sweet liquid lubricating her parched throat and she let her black hair fall over one shoulder and stroked—then realized she was the only grown female there. The mother had yelled No and Estrella should have been safely tucked away like the other women of the camp because the moon and earth and sun's alignment was a powerful thing. Unborn children lurking in their bodies were in danger of having their lips bitten just like the hare on the moon if nothing was done to protect them. Is that what you want, the mother yelled, a child born sin labios? Without a mouth? And Estrella looked out to the barn. Behind her something dunked water, and Estrella listened. A frog splashed perhaps, or someone skipped a rock above the water of the irrigation ditch.

She scratched a foot, a finger digging into her boot, no socks. Her knees. He saw her knees. She preened her hair and it gave Alejo the idea that it was a luxury for her to sit and rake her long hair, to fill her own nostrils with the newly washed scent of boiled chrysanthemum. She had tilted her head up to drink again and her hair fell back and the moon reappeared, puncturing the coppery night with its ever-glowing belly. The craters of the moon punched out the shape of a hare.

Estrella bobbled her knees and passed the bottle to Alejo, her extended arm obscuring the moon just as the earth's shadow had done a few minutes before, and he took the bottle and finished the drink. He dug in his pocket and felt for the stone.

The crickets once again blasted from the vacant field, their chirping drowning the rustle of the trees. The whistling halted. A few yawning men started back down toward the bonfire, the children chasing behind them.

—I'm sorry, Alejo said.

—For what, she replied.

—For whatever I said that made you mad.

—It's not you, Estrella said, and jumped down from the fence.

—You sure?

—Yeah, and Estrella pointed to the bottle because she wanted to tell him how good she felt but didn't know how to build the house of words she could invite him into. That was real good, she said, and they looked at one another and waited. Build rooms as big as barns. He held the neck of the empty bottle tight and traced the thick spout with his thumb. Wide-open windows where she could put candlelights and people from across the way would point at the glow and not feel so alone in the night. Give it here, she said, and pointed to the bottle and Alejo thought that perhaps she wanted the deposit and gladly handed it to her. She dunked her top lip on the spout and placed her thumb near her lip and grooved a breath into the hollow and it sounded full of longing. Estrella blew some more deep and low notes, her thumb directing the flow of air.

—Pretty good, he said, and she returned the bottle. When he placed his lips and blew, nothing came of it.

—Like that, and she took his warm thumb slightly in her trembling hand, Here.

—Here? Like this? He blew and a weak note emerged which made her smile but embarrassed him.

—See you tomorrow, she said as if she believed it.

—Yea, okay, he replied, very pleased. See you around, See you.

She started across the vacant corral, buried in the hip-high mustard grass, her boot chafing against her bare ankle bone. Estrella felt a pinch and her finger lingered on her lips and she became suddenly startled by the moon and the harelip boy and the No of the mother. To her relief, she heard wind groaning over the mouth of the bottle, notes far and wayward in the night. She stopped and turned. Alejo receded to the camp, all the while blowing notes as deep as a basement

71

until all she could see was the blue bottle floating toward the yellow glow of the bonfire.

The mother had covered the windows of the bungalow with newspapers and a paste made of flour and water. She asked for Perfecto's keys, forbid Estrella from going outside. What do you want with the keys, Perfecto asked, and the mother placed the keys in the pocket of her apron, near her belly, without answering.

White butterflies and golden wasps and green and brown lace flies swooped and hovered before her as she trudged across the brittle thistles to meet Perfecto. Her shoes were caked with mud and laced above her trousers dusty from a full day's work. Estrella wiped her forehead with the back of a sleeve. The late afternoon skies sheened a hubcap silver over the barn and the orchards, and a flock of ducks flew above her like an arrowhead, their beaks and necks dipping in flight. Her body slouched, and when she remembered, or when she saw her own shadow against the tall grasses, she straightened her shoulders and pushed her chest out. A few stray ducks pumped their wings.

She finally spotted Perfecto. He leaned on a sideboard of the corral fence and waited where the mother said he would be waiting because it was urgent and he needed to talk with her right after work. The skullcap of his balding head glistened with sweat and she could see him glancing in the direction of the peach orchards.

She heard the faint buzzsaw engine of a biplane as she approached the fence. Rather than straddle herself on the top board as she had done a few months back, she found a loose board and pulled one end down. She climbed over and raised the worn wood plank up again into the notch of nail. She waited for him to say something.

Perfecto cleaned his thumbnail with a corner of a matchbook. He thought of the matchbook, then of a cigarette, and then of a smoldering heat burning on the bare skin of his head.

—Can you help tear down the barn? Perfecto asked. He was not a man who minced words. His hands were big for such a wiry body, with veins that surfaced like swollen roots. The twins loved to play with his hands. Whenever they caught Perfecto sitting, they would join him like bookends and place his hands, palms down, on their laps and entertain themselves by pressing the veins in, then watching the veins gradually surface from his skin like running streams on parched land.

—You listening to what I'm asking?

—Weren't they gonna spray the orchards next week? Estrella asked matter-of-factly, and pointed to the biplane which dusted the peach trees not far from the barn. She tilted her head for a better look. Such a big noise for such a small plane.

—Since when do they do what they say? Perfecto put the matchbook in his front shirt pocket and waited for the noise of the plane to lessen before speaking again.

He leaned his elbows on a side board of the fence as Alejo had done a few nights before. Well?

—Makes a lot of noise, don't it?

—I need for you to help me.

—I thought I had no business in the barn, Estrella replied. She walked over to its shade. I thought you said it was dangerous.

—It means extra money.

—How come me?

—If I get Gumecindo to help tear it down, I gotta pay him.

—How 'bout Alejo? she asked, and Perfecto kicked pebbles before answering. His boot was splitting at the toe.

—Same thing. Less for your mama.

Perfecto rubbed his head. He had forgotten to put his hat on and the sun beamed on his baldness. It angered him just thinking of the wide rim hat with its darkened sweatring around the crown, sitting on a nail next to the door instead of on his head. This was the third time he had forgotten the hat. Se me va la onda. What was he thinking?

—Are you gonna help or no?

—It's not fair, Estrella said. Except for the dress she'd pulled over her work clothes, she resembled a young man, standing in the barn's shadow. She looked up at the barn as she had done when they first arrived, and tried to imagine herself with the ball of a hammer, pulling the resistant long rusted nails out of the woodsheet walls. The nails would screech and the wood would moan and she would pull the veins out and the woodsheet wall would collapse like a toothless mouth. Nothing would be left except a hole in the baked dirt so wide it would make one wonder how anything could be so empty.

Is that what happens? Estrella thought, people just use you until you're all used up, then rip you into pieces when they're finished using you? She scratched under her hat, the day's sweat working its way into her scalp. She should have taken a drink from the cooling bucket of water before coming.

The blue bottle and the brand cola and pulp of the moon over the cedar shakes of the barn wouldn't have been so strong if she wasn't so thirsty, so hungry, so tired she wanted to curl up in the straw and shut the trapdoors, let the dust settle in the dark and close her eyes.

But there was no wind today, and when she noticed the silence of the birds in the quiet trees, she realized the plane had stopped its fumigation.

—Why does the barn have to go down?

—Someone died there, Perfecto said. This was true. This one was not a lie.

—In there?

—It's no business of ours.

—I don't believe you.

—Why do you think people stay away?

—The harelip boy comes here all the time.

75

—You must be dreaming.

—Who told you someone died?

—It's no secret.

—I'm not scared, Perfecto, she lied.

—You should be.

Perfecto Flores thought it best not to get angry. He removed his bifocals and scratched his ashen scruffy chin, the back of his loose neck skin, then slipped his bifocals on again.

—I need you to help.

—No. I can't do it.

He turned and left Estrella looking at the barn, her face blanked out under the shadow of her hat.

Alejo had not guessed the biplane was so close until its gray shadow crossed over him like a crucifix, and he ducked into the leaves. The biplane circled, banking steeply over the trees and then released the shower of white pesticide.

—What the . . . ? They're spraying! But Alejo couldn't hear Gumecindo's response because the drone of the motor like the snapping of rubber bands drowned out his words.

—Run! Alejo screamed, struggling to get himself down from the tree, Get the fuck outta here!

Gumecindo dropped the sacks and ran, jumping over irrigation pumps, crunching the flesh of rotting peaches, running just ahead of the cross shadow.

Alejo slid through the bushy branches, the tangled

twigs scratching his face, and he was ready to jump when he felt the mist. He shut his eyes tight to the mist of black afternoon. At first it was just a slight moisture until the poison rolled down his face in deep sticky streaks. The lingering smell was a scent of ocean salt and beached kelp until he inhaled again and could detect under the innocence the heavy chemical choke of poison. Air clogged in his lungs and he thought he was just holding his breath, until he tried exhaling but couldn't, which meant he couldn't breathe. He panicked when he realized he was choking, clamped his neck with one hand, feeling his Adam's apple against his palm, but still held onto a branch tightly with the other, afraid he would fall long and hard, like the insects did. He swallowed finally and the spit in his throat felt like balls of scratchy sand. Was this punishment for his thievery? He was sorry Lord, so sorry.

Alejo's head spun and he shut his stinging eyes tighter to regain balance. But a hole ripped in his stomach like a match to paper, spreading into a deeper and bigger black hole that wanted to swallow him completely. He knew he would vomit. His clothes were dampened through, then the sheet of his skin absorbed the chemical and his whole body began to cramp from the shrinking pull of his skin squeezing against his bones.

He wheezed and almost fell, and if it wasn't for the fact that he was determined not to fall, he would have tumbled like the ripe peaches hitting the ground with a hard thud. His body swung forward and he caught himself by hitching on to a branch and he scratched his face against a mesh of leaves. As the rotary motor of the biplane approached again, he closed his eyes and imagined sinking into the tar pits.

He thought first of his feet sinking, sinking to his knee joints, swallowing his waist and torso, the pressure of tar squeezing his chest and crushing his ribs. Engulfing his skin up to his chin, his mouth, his nose, bubbled air. Black bubbles erasing him. Finally the eyes. Blankness. Thousands of bones, the bleached white marrow of bones. Splintered bone pieced together by wire to make a whole, surfaced bone. No fingerprint or history, bone. No lava stone. No story or family, bone. And when he awoke from the darkness of the tar, he was looking up into the canopy of peach trees, his forehead a swamp of purple blood and bruise and hair, and into the face of his cousin.

Perfecto contemplated the forked path. Under the shade of some trees, he bent his wiry limbs, an old weathervane of a body, the rusted axis of his knees rattling like pivots in the wind. He raked his throat of phlegm, spit it out. Jittery flies settled on his shoulders to work their forelegs together while a yellow jacket wasp tested his ear. The winds shifted and he breathed in a faint trace of saltwater and coughed.

Perfecto desired to return home. To his real home, not the bungalow. This desire became as urgent as the money he brought in for Petra's family. He kept forgetting his hat, stumbling over his memories like a child learning to walk; as if in seventy-three years he had traveled too long a distance to keep himself steady and able and willing. What would happen if he forgot his way home?

This morning, he awoke next to a young woman and it thrilled him because this was the woman who he had loved boldly in the canyon right under the cataract eyes of God. Without the church's legal signature, he had pushed his trousers down to his ankles and sat, the hot limestone against his bare buttocks, and reassured her that this was love, trust him, and he had pulled her into him right under the open sky and sun and cloudy eyes. She had straddled him, her knees folding open like a waxed cactus flower, her heels digging into the small of his back, the grind of the stone, his face under the cotton of her dress, the smell of peeled cucumbers, fleshy red opuntia fruit. The glossy semen had flashed out of him and into her and out of her and down his thigh and had evaporated on the limestone like clear water.

This morning he toyed between the crescent cloves of her shoulder blades and she turned to him and it wasn't Mercedes of another life, and he awoke a second time and the scent of garlic startled him. He got up and didn't know where he was and he fumbled for his bifocals and he rattled out of the bungalow in his calico drawers, stumbling to his car. He looked in the sideview mirror of the station wagon and saw that his hair was not full black as it had been in the dream, and his naked skin was not tight taut as he had seen himself with Mercedes of some forty years ago. He tried to rack his brain, shake out the contents of his memories to remember who he was and who he wasn't.

Mealybug beetles dripped like crisp curls on Perfecto's knees, then fell to the ground, and he studied the black beetles, the armor of their backs, their legs jetting and jerking. He remembered their firstborn, the color of a plum. Perfecto poked the beetles with a finger. Mercedes buried her head in shame at her failure but did not bury her accusatory stare. She told him the women hadn't schooled her in the ritual of birthing because it was against *his* church; to know the ceremonies would be to know demons and heathens. She wanted no part of his God after that. But Perfecto knew better; there was no absolution for their love in the canyon. It was about travesties, about transgression. It had nothing to do with rituals. A few lace wing flies jutted across the soft soils with furious flapping. They had other children, but the lesson of that one life came at too high a price.

They returned the blue silenced baby to the soil days later, without the blessing of the priest, a plastic wreath wrapped with fake flower stems. Only a baby's blanket was left. Mercedes washed and folded and buried the blanket in the basket of her own things. But no one believed him when he claimed that the sweet-sour baby smell still clung to the blanket. He could not find words or colors to describe the smells. He could only describe what the blanket *smelled like*: citrus and mint, rose-water, sometimes cloves. Even years later, while Mercedes' cancer burrowed into her chest, Perfecto would take the blanket out of the basket, and press the cloth to his nose. Each time a child grew and left, he inhaled, and when Mercedes died that crazy night centuries ago, the scent of pure cloves fired the memory of such a short life into his nostrils and rushed to his lungs, flashing his heart till it pumped so fast it made his head spin and his eyes water endlessly. No one believed him, but he swore year after year he could still smell the living scent of their first-born baby.

Perfecto coughed into his fist, and his nose began to run and he blew his nose and sneezed again. Flies tumbled like leaves from the bushy trees, dropping onto his shoulders and then onto the ground. Perfecto slowly rose to his feet and pulled out his handkerchief again and he jammed it against his nose. Dying insects lay on the soil everywhere.

In the morning light, Alejo saw mud and tar under his nails and this frightened him. He felt like splintered and chipped sea shells embedded in layers of the desert rock, so far away from the ocean. Something had gone wrong. The sea had receded without him. The side-boards of the truck clacked like broken dishes and the noise made him start:

—¡Gumecindo!

—¿Qué traes?

—I'm not feeling well.

—'Mano, the bump on your head looks bad.

—I hurt, man.

—Don't go to work today.

—Just help me on the truck. I'll be okay.

The piscadores looked at one another, stared at Alejo who sat embracing his belly and they squeezed away from him as if bad luck was as contagious as any illness.

The thick smell of chemical and saltwater had not abandoned his nostrils and Alejo felt as if he reeked. His mouth salivated and when he spit over the sideboard, Ricky did as well.

—What happened to you? Estrella pointed to his bruised and scraped forehead, You gonna be okay? The tall gray shadows of the eucalyptus trees flashed on his face as they drove along the road. There were three trucks in a row this time, bumping along to another part of the ranch.

—I fell.

—You oughta be more careful.

—It's already too late, qué no Star? He touched the dried scab on his forehead and when he winced with the pain, he caught a hint of solace in her face. It's just too late.

The desire to return home was now a tumor lodged under the muscle of Perfecto's heart and getting larger

82

with every passing day. It caused him to lose his breath, to close his eyes in the middle of the grapevines when the sun was high above the sky.

Perfecto lived a travesty of laws. He knew nothing of their source but it seemed his very existence contradicted the laws of others, so that everything he did like eat and sleep and work and love was prohibited. He didn't want to waste what little time he had left. With or without Estrella's help, he committed himself to tearing the barn down. The money was essential to get home before home became so distant, he wouldn't be able to remember his way back.

He narrowed his eyes against the glare of the sun. Feeling an unspeakable sadness, he sat under the vines for relief and he could hear his heart pumping in his ears. He staked the soil between his workshoes with his knife again and again. The soil dulled the sharpness of his blade as it did his own life.

Later that same week, two piscadores fainted. The portable radio with a thunderbolt of twisted wire hanger for an antenna sizzled a report of 109 degrees Fahrenheit. Radio Cali, Rosarito, Baja California. A woman had called in and requested the D.J. play Las Mañanitas for her husband who turned twenty-one and the D.J. joked about their sex lives. Piscadores placed their burritos on the dented hood of the Ford pickup truck to heat them. The drivers pitched tarpaulin tents and tables for a noon break and those weak from the sun were given apricot and peach crates to sit on.

They crowded under the shade, sitting on crates, or on their haunches, while others soaked their bandannas in water, then looped the wet cloth around their stinging necks. The sun burned their feet, their heads, their eyes. A young boy cried, his cheeks smeared with snot and dirt, and his mother hushed him with water and sugar, then wiped his face with the corner of her workshirt. Another woman sat on the step of the pickup and nursed her baby, a diaper over her modest breast. The plump, bare feet of the baby wiggled from under the cover and Estrella touched the pealike toes and the toes curled and this made her smile. To Estrella, this woman seemed so young. Her own age maybe? The woman looked away.

Estrella relinquished her crate to the Señora Josefina. Ayy, she wheezed out as she sat. Ayyyy. The drivers passed water in paper cups and when the Foreman left, a few passed out white leaflets with black eagles on them. Estrella received one, folded it in half carefully and placed it in her back pocket for later reading. Her eyes hurt too much.

A commercial spit out a man's voice announcing Gigante Mueblería and easy credit porque hay un especial de sillones "Lazy Boy." A caller asked the D.J. ¿Cuál es el criterio que usa la migra pa' reconocer mojados? Canned laughter. Whose back was wetter, asked the D.J., those who crossed the river, or those who crossed the ocean? The caller didn't get the joke and the jingle of another commercial cued in and Estrella thought of swimming and water and ice.

No one had claimed the shade under one of the trucks. The truck leaked oil and hot water from the radiator and so Estrella inched her back against the gravel from the rear. The truck was elevated so that if she wanted, she could move sideways, but opted to lay on her back, her hands behind her head. Her shoes sprouted from under the rear brake light. She bent one leg and her idle knee touched the muffler pipe.

The recline of her body against the baked earth made her drowsy and she yawned. She lay staring at the Ford's blackened entrails which went in and out like a knot of pipes, then followed a long rusted pipe between the front and rear bumpers. She turned to see muddied boots and tennis shoes and sandals crunching back and forth, someone spilling water, paper cups and foil crumpled on the ground. She could not tell men from women by their shoes. Someone turned the portable volume to ten and Los Panchos sang out a sweet bolero loudly. The D.J. invited his listeners to sing along.

The shuffling of various shoes moved to make space in the crowded slab of shade for a couple to dance. Estrella heard laughter and voices hooting at the dancers, and she watched them slide to the tune of picking guitars, if only for a minute and then the shoes closed in once again.

His big high-tops approached the truck and she

could clearly see the thick gray rubber soles against the black canvas, just as clearly as she could see the oil greased thick on the shock absorbers. His baseball cap dropped and he bent to pick it up and she saw his eyes, his forehead still black and blue. His face disappeared and she followed his big shoes as far as she could see. She could hear his body sliding from the front bumper.

—Watch for the oil. She felt obliged to warn him.

—Too late. I got some on my pants.

—So sorry.

—You know where oil comes from? he asked in a whisper, as if the sun had sucked out even the energy to speak in a normal tone. Now the music of the radio was barely audible over the talk of the piscadores. The D.J. joked with a man whose wife threw him out of the house. There was more canned laughter. Someone changed the station and a kaleidoscope of sounds resolved itself into the tuba clank of Banda music.

—Probably a leak from the motor.

—I don't mean that.

—Why you asking me?

—If we don't have oil, we don't have gasoline.

—Good. We'd stay put then.

—Stuck, more like it. Stuck.

—Aren't we now? Estrella flattened her knee. She crossed her legs at her ankles, one pant cuff over another. Someone whistled to the song.

—Ever heard of tar pits? he asked.

—Peach pits, maybe. She heard him laugh.

—Millions of years ago, the dead animals and plants fell to the bottom of the sea.

—You like to talk, don't you?

—Imagine bones at the bottom of the sea . . .

—If you say so. Estrella yawned. She found it hard to imagine the cool silence of the ocean floor when her feet were itching with swelling sweat and she could feel the constraint of her shoes as if her feet were bound. But smell it yes, she smelled the kelp.

—Bones and rocks and leaves. Falling. Slowly.

Estrella studied the way the tire tread actually had a lacy diamond pattern like the scarf doily the mother spread under Jesucristo. *Falling*. She noticed the color white had faded out of the imprinted word GOOD-YEAR. *Slowly*. His words were hypnotic over the hum of radio waves.

—The bones lay in the seabed for millions of years. That's how it was. Makes sense don't it, bones becoming tar oil? Estrella felt Alejo's hand take hers and she could feel the wet of sweat rolling down the side of her breast. She was used to bodies, those of her sisters and brothers, pressing themselves against her while they slept; or the body of the mother whenever she looped her arms around her without embarrassment at the strangest times, like while Estrella bit into a tortilla at dinner, or when she returned from the outdoor toilet. Estrella had even become used to Maxine's bologna smell when she lay next to her while reading *Millie the Model*. But this skin was different, this heat was different, this scent.

She became aware of his body shifting in the gravel, imagined where his face was, where the words came from. She could feel the hairs of her arm stand erect, and could feel the space between her shoulder blades molting sweat. She heard him swallow a dry swallow as if he needed a drink of water then heard him inhale, his breath pulling in streams of hot air. Estrella tried to distract herself by studying the nuts and grimy bolts and how tightly they were screwed onto the tire. She pulled her hand away gently to touch the bolts and rolled the blackened tar between her fingers.

—Tar oil? You say tar oil, huh?

—Once, when I picked peaches, I heard screams. It reminded me of the animals stuck in the tar pits.

—Did people? Did people ever get stuck?

—Only one, Alejo replied, in the La Brea tar pits, they found some human bones. A young girl.

They were quiet. Estrella felt him take her hand again, her fingers soiled with the tar grease, and she closed her eyes. She did not resist, unaware of where he was taking her or how. Alejo carefully smoothed her fingers flat as if unfolding a map. His mouth pressed against the center of her palm and his lips, which felt as dry as baking soda, lingered until the heat of his air welded into the cup of her hand. Her fingers closed on his chin gently like the tentacles of a sea anemone. He then pressed his cheek against the nakedness of her palm and his bristles tickled and she smiled in her darkness, until Alejo kissed her again, but this time longer, damp and pleadingly and still. Her oiled handprint, the shape of her fingers, imprinted onto his face. And that was all he had to do.

Estrella lay very still, very quiet, her eyes closed tightly, trying not to think of Exits and Entrances, of Stop signs and Yields. She fisted her hand with a grasp as tight as a heart and then slipped her hand in her front pocket. He was quiet and she wanted to blank out the hunger and so she tried to think of tar oil so black, it swallowed the radio and the baby's plump toes and the shoes crunching all around the edges of her life. She uncrossed her ankles.

Estrella ran, feeling the breeze on her face. If Maxine were here, she would have run to her, but instead she ran as fast as her clumsy boots allowed to the barn. She gripped the door frame of the barn and entered. She breathed in the musk hot scent of manure. The lace of webs which hung on the rafters fluttered softly. Beams of sunlight stabbed through the high ceilings and slanting walls, like swords in a magician's box crisscrossing each other. Estrella couldn't resist. She cupped her hands on one of the sunbeams, the motes of dust swirling upward, while the beam shot downward. She caught the flow of sun, felt the laser heat slowly penetrate her palms he had kissed, saw the blood of her body, a brilliant reddish pink rose, and she laughed. The safety pins on the cuffs of her sleeves glimmered like diamonds. She heard the creak of old wood complaining, and she heard the owls, their nervous claws ticking against the slope of the gabled roof and it was then she realized she was not alone. She looked around for the harelip boy, but saw no one.

Now unafraid, she walked to the center of the barn where the chain suspended in an almost unnatural way. Everything else belonged: the stalls, the thick scent of damp hay, the straw spread on the flattened earth, the rusted pitchfork leaning against the deep grooves of weathered sheet wood, everything except the chain. She flipped her head back to stare at the ceiling and her hat tumbled to the floor, her hair tumbling to her shoulders. Why was the chain there? Was it part of a grain shaft of some kind? She noticed a trapdoor, squared by the sunlight near where the chain hooked the ceiling. She took hold of its end, yanked it like a bell ringer, lightly at first to test it, then jerked it with all her muscle, then jumped out of the way in case the chain was not hooked securely. She crunched her hat beneath her shoes. The chain barely resisted. It chinked in suspension as it did the first time she saw it. As she bent to pick up her hat, Estrella noticed her hands. Once filled with light, her palms were now tainted with brick red rust.

Three

*F*lorente of the islands informed Gumecindo that his cousin Alejo had a sickness they called daño of the fields. This was not sunstroke or a flu, but worse. Alejo could no longer stand upright without feeling faint, his body weak from bouts of diarrhea and vomiting. He stayed behind day after day until Gumecindo didn't know what to do.

—He needs to be home, Perfecto advised. He pushed his bifocals up the bridge of his nose for a better look at the swerving worms surfacing from the soil imprints of his shoes. Perfecto had not seen them drop from the sky so the maggots must have burrowed out of the very earth he stood on.

—¿Mande? asked Gumecindo, What did you say?

—He needs to be home, Perfecto repeated. He slowly twisted the tip of his boot into the larvae.

—But he can't even move.

—Maybe all he needs is rest, offered Petra. She pulled a plastic lid off a green can of coffee.

—But we gotta get home soon, before school starts.

—Give it more time.

—The buses are already leaving.

—They can't wait?

—I don't know.

The mottled afternoon clouds drifted like smoke over the crackling cooking pit and Petra, who dropped three heaping spoons of ground coffee into the steaming coffeepot, then sprinkled cool water to make the grinds fall to the bottom. A breeze gently lifted the scent of garlic and woodsmoke and fluttered Petra's apron strings while the twin Cookie darted up the steps of the porch. All of this made Perfecto feel a little better and he stopped digging his boot into the soil.

—Did Florente say it's catchable? asked Petra, retying her duck-print apron strings into a floppy, looped knot.

—It's not. He's seen it lots of times.

Perfecto studied Gumecindo's worried face, so young it was as bare of whiskers as Ricky's. Perhaps, some time ago, in another country, he must have been that young too.

—How old are you? Perfecto asked, because with the worms and the sky and all, he needed to know.

—Fifteen.

—¿Y tu primo Alejo?

—Sixteen, almost.

—Almost? Perfecto sighed. He took a zinc bucket and turned it over. Sit here, he said, tapping it lightly and Gumecindo obeyed. What can I tell you?

—I knew something was coming down, Gumecindo said. He sat and hung his head and shook it, remembering the premonition of the screams. I just knew it. I could feel it in my bones.

—When you feel it that deep, you should listen, Petra added. She polished an enamel cup with a dish towel. Cookie jumped off the porch and ran and tugged on Petra's duck apron and Petra turned the twin's face inward against her belly and tried smoothing down the tangled mess of her daughter's hair. She automatically searched for the other twin because to see one twin was to see one shoe. Perla sat crosslegged on the porch, studying the trek of a red ladybug which crawled over her wrist and around to her palm.

—¡Deja ai! Petra yelled, but Perla prompted the metallic bug with a fingernail. Cookie ran back to the porch.

—Have you eaten? Perfecto asked Gumecindo, but the clouds in Gumecindo's head drifted in and out of *can't wait*, and shrouded Perfecto's voice and he didn't answer.

Petra wrapped the towel around the arm of the coffee pot. She poured a cup and placed the pot back on the hot grate and offered coffee to Gumecindo. He took it with a pensive nod.

—Do they taste crunchy? Cookie asked, now holding a handful of ladybugs.

—¡Deja ai! Petra grabbed Cookie's wrist and shook it. The black spots on the bugs' red glossy backs split in two and leapt off. Petra knew she could never turn her back on the children. Maybe we should bring him here, Petra said. She attempted to lift Cookie but felt the strain on her legs. Go play, she ordered Cookie, but the twin scanned the ground for the ladybugs.

—You think so? Perfecto asked. I mean . . . Petra settled on the crate and rubbed the inside of her right knee. She would double the garlic.

—If we don't take care of each other, who would take care of us? Petra asked. We have to look out for our own.

Perfecto felt uncomfortable discussing Alejo in his cousin's presence, but Gumecindo was lost in the dark of his coffee. He guessed that Gumecindo was already on the bus going home.

—He's sick, Petra. Sicker than any yerba, any prayer could cure.

—It's not good to leave people behind.

—You don't understand.

—I feel it in my bones.

—You can't even stand up, Perfecto continued, punctuating the fact with a trembling wave of one big hand. He glanced at her veins which bubbled thicker into a color of a deep bruise when she stood on her feet too long. What makes you think you can help him?

—What makes you think I can't?

—You have enough on your hands.

—If Arnulfo or Ricky or my hija got sick, I would want someone to take care of them, wouldn't you? She stopped rubbing.

—This is different, Perfecto said, lowering his voice.

—How? How is it different than us?

—It's too much, he answered, too much.

—One never knows what obstacles God puts before us as a test.

—A test? Perfecto asked increduously. The coffee overboiled and singed the flames.

—You know what I mean.

—You're crazy, I tell you.

Petra stood up. With the corner of her apron, she wrapped the handle of the coffee pot and removed it from the fire.

Perfecto shook his head repeatedly.

—I can't allow it.

—It's not in our hands.

—I can't allow it. He noticed a puncture in the ribbed clouds which floated right toward him. For a moment, he felt as if the hand of God was going to reach right through the hole and pull him up to the heavens. He glanced down and the maggots looked like white specks against the chocolate soil. His chest ached.

—Not now, he pleaded, Not now.

—What's the matter with you?

—I say you can't!

—Tell me to go to the devil, Petra replied, tell me I'm crazy. But don't tell me that. Don't tell me I can't. Petra ambled to the crate and sat a second time and smoothed the apron on her lap and X-ed her arms over her chest like two planks boarding up a window.

With the help of Perfecto Flores, Gumecindo carried his cousin into the bungalow and lay him on the pile of blankets which made up a bed. After Petra propped a pillow for him, Alejo already felt better. He had been left alone for many days while the others went off to work, leaving him breathing in the smell of foul socks and loneliness. And Alejo thought if he was going to die, he did not want to die alone. His body muscles spasmed every time he moved in the slightest way, and all the ache rushed to his head as he came in and out of the deep well of days.

Petra brought some rice water for his runs and scooped the back of his head up, put the cup to his lips. He could barely drink the pasty gray water and the scent of his illness was a fog of sweat and rotting garbage. Later he felt a cool object, and opened his eyes to see Petra rubbing a hen's egg on his bare stomach while she muttered prayers to herself. He struggled to turn his head, watch her crack the same egg in two, then pour it in a saucer, watched her study the yellow yolk, after which she placed the egg and saucer behind his head and left it there, and then he closed his eyes.

In a daze of sleep and ache and loneliness, he felt Perfecto struggling to pull his pants off, saw Petra near him with buckets of water, and only realized when he felt the soothing warm water between his thighs, that he had soiled himself and they were cleaning him and he felt too pitiful to be ashamed. He hoped Star was far away.

That same day, Alejo slept contentedly for hours. When he awoke it was dark, and the cool scent of orchard resin refreshed him and he felt better. He listened to the sound of night crickets coming from the open window, the raspy breathing of children that he missed whenever he was away from home. Sleeping in a room full of children was different than sleeping in a room full of men. The smells and noises and dreams were different. He noticed Star's back next to him. One button on the back of her floral dress had slipped from its mouth and he moved closer to her to feel the comfort of that unburied patch of skin. She, accustomed to the legs and arms of her brothers and sisters, pushed herself against him to fill any crevices between their bodies that would allow the chill to enter. There was a distinct scent to her of woodsmoke and sweat and soil, but also a sweetness like Eagles' condensed milk that he inhaled from the back of her neck. She turned, a breath coming from between her lips, her face looking as if she took her sleep seriously.

A sleeping face looked so different than one awake.

Her eyelashes were long and thick black against a complexion brown like wheat bread crust, and except for the blemishes on her forehead, her skin was smooth and soft when he touched her cheek. Drowsy, she fanned her face. Alejo pulled closer to her, rested near her chest and with her lulling breathing against his cheek, he became convinced he would not die after all.

Last Monday, Perfecto had watched Petra stop kneading the dough on the table. She looked out at the eucalyptus trees thinking of what, he didn't know, and her stare made him think for a moment that the trees were whispering his secret to her. Could she know what he thought? Could she tell by the way he took to looking for extra jobs? Could she hear it in the clanking bells of the train crossing? But she broke her stare, continued kneading the white dough for the dinner tortillas.

The Thursday before he had dreamt of illness, his veins like irrigation canals clogged with dying insects, twitching on their backs, their little twig legs jerking. The following night he dreamt of Mercedes calling to him in the ridiculous frilly dress she was buried in. His dreams were never in color. Perfecto, don't you remember us? she whispered in sepia tones. Or was it his baby? It was the memories that bound his spirit to his native soil. He knew the ghosts were working in the dream world to tell him something, yet each night that he lay next to Petra, he prayed that the spirits would keep quiet and let him enjoy the tenderness of a woman who wore an aura of garlic as brilliant as the aura circling La Virgen. What more could he have asked of the spirits? But it was too late, too late. He was too old to support this family, and who did he think he was, and on Saturday, he dreamt of keys and the moon and that Petra was pregnant.

There was no denying the insect signs that warned him. Even Petra had said it: when you feel it that deep, listen. The final sign was the young man Alejo. He could feel the boy's death under his bare feet as he carried him up the porch and into their house. It was that close.

Alejo felt a mosquito buzzing and lifted his hand to swat it away. He swiped his hand to his face, his head too groggy to open his eyes. Finally, irritated by the mosquito, he opened his eyes to see Cookie tickling his nose with a white thread. He turned his face to the window, and thought he was seeing double, for he saw Perla studying the pock marks and the stubble of cheek that felt like sandpaper when she touched it.

Perfecto wiped the crusty terminal posts of the car battery with a soiled rag he kept under the driver's seat for checking the oil. He removed the vent hole caps and sniffed for the corrosive smell of sulfuric acid, then replaced the caps and slammed shut the hood of the station wagon and threw the blackened rag on the front seat. There was no doubt that the wagon needed a new battery. The acid had become so diluted with water, the smell was gone, and this made the starter skip like a spoon scraping against metal. Now it was only a matter of time. He pulled his kerchief from his back pocket and wiped away grease from between his fingers as he walked toward the bungalow. The salvaging of the barn would bring in some good money. At least he could purchase a new battery and have enough left over to leave them some.

Ricky and Arnulfo collected firewood, and when they broke into swordplay, he called to them to quit the monkey business and carry the wood to the pit. He thought of his own children, grown now with children of their own, and wondered where they were, which side of the border they settled in, wondered how he had managed to stray so far away and for so long.

The twins ran to him, grabbed a thick hand each, their hands fleshy and moist. At first Perfecto recoiled his hands because he no longer liked the feel of the warm little knots of fingers tying into his; but they anchored a hand each anyway, clamping their grasp and laughing. They chattered together excitedly but with different words, tried to tell him that Alejo had opened his eyes and told them to go away, just in those words, like that, Go away, and they were very pleased. The twins tugged Perfecto Flores to the porch. Petra emerged with a hint of a smile at his forgetfulness, her two hands holding the rim of his hat again. He tried not to see her, passed her to enter the bungalow.

Petra knew the capricious black lines on a map did little to reveal the hump and tear of the stitched pavement which ascended to the morning sun and through the trees and no trees, and became a swollen main street and then a loose road once again outside the hamlets that appeared as splat dots on paper. They had travelled by foot, in and out of the orchards, until they reached the main highway and Petra could feel the heat pulsating from the asphalt. The oil of the pavement mirrored like puddles of fresh rainwater though it hadn't rained in months. The family stood in file on the thistle belt of road and rested.

Under the strutting powerlines, Estrella sat on her haunches. The floral fabric of her dress was thin from repeated washes and the reddish blue violets paled against the searing sunlight. She sunk her white thumbnail into the pavement and slowly sliced a sliver on the melted tar. Not far across the highway, the rickety store stood as desirous as a drink of water.

—It's real hot, Estrella said.

—So tell us something we don't know, Ricky replied. The rubber of his shoe stuck with thistle thorns which were planted around the fenceless edges of the orchards to discourage roadside thievery. He carefully plucked off a few.

—Should we wait? Arnulfo asked, looking down the slithery road. It looked as flat as a crushed, dried snake.

—Wait for what? snapped Petra in a tone that was tired, and therefore mean. She lay her forehead on her palm. The only relief from the reaming sun came at twilight and twilight seemed as far away as the store. A lime green Bermuda with a white top and white wall tires rolled off the road and under the awning of the store's single gas pump and braked and two people got off.

—Vámanos, Petra decided.

Estrella heaved Perla on her shoulders with firm instructions, *Keep your manitas outta my eyeballs, gordita*, she said, and the twin nodded like a jiggle doll on the backseat of a car. Plump legs dangled on Estrella's chest and the twin's moist palms rested on her forehead.

—Maybe we should wait, Arnulfo meekly repeated. A Ford pickup with a dented headlight rambled by and honked and the blast frightened him.

—After this one, Petra said, pointing to an Allied Moving truck which whisked by with such incredible speed, it forced the hems of dresses up and shirts to fly open. Estrella lifted Cookie's buttocks and the twin clamped her legs around her waist.

Petra looked both ways. A convoy of vehicles appeared from nowhere, whipping their faces with grainy wind.

—After this one, Petra said again.

Cookie tightened her grasp. Estrella followed the

clicking of the mother's rubber sandals. The twins were heavier than usual. Her neck strained from Perla's clamped hold. *Let go a little.* The thistle thorns on her shoes felt like cleats as she sprinted across the asphalt in short, precise steps. *You're not gonna fall.*

When they reached the gas pump, Estrella lowered Cookie immediately and slid Perla off her shoulders and the sudden release of weight made her dizzy. Patches of sweat pasted her back and saturated the violets into deep purple flowers. She slipped under the tinted awning, her shadow dissolving like lard in a hot skillet. The driver of the Bermuda cocked the trigger of the dispenser and the old gas pump began rotating clackety numbers. The vapors of the gasoline idled in the air.

—Next time, Petra wagged her finger at the twins: Next time, you two will have to walk. The twins cowered behind Estrella. Huercos fregados, she whispered.

Petra crossed her arms and looked at the Bermuda's plump seats. The white plush carpeting was so white, it was obvious no one ate in the car. She envied the car, then envied the landlord of the car who could travel from one splat dot to another. She thought him a man who knew his neighbors well, who returned to the same bed, who could tell where the schools and where the stores were, and where the Nescafé coffee jars in the stores were located, and payday always came at the end of the week. The gas dispenser triggered off and Bermuda man removed it.

The boys had not crossed the highway. Ricky

plucked the thorns from his shoe. The man snapped a blue paper towel from a silver box and buffed the chrome of his car.

—Should I go get them? Estrella asked.

—You always gonna carry them on your back? Petra was angry. Another semitrailer roared past and their dresses fluttered between their knees. ¡AHORA MISMO! Petra yelled to the boys after the truck was safely out of ears reach. Pronto! and she pierced her finger in the air. But the dried snake frightened the boys. Arnulfo remembered how they had found a snake. So perfectly crushed was the snake by the tire of a huge semi, Ricky couldn't even scrape the slithered body off the pavement with a butterknife.

Petra raised her voice so that there would be little doubt in their minds: PRONTO! Or you'll get a chanclaso! The Bermuda man looked at her over the hood of his lime green car, and the sun reflected wavy green on his face. Petra wore mismatched clothes and had chosen the clothes for their blues because blue was a cool color against the hot tempered sun and that was why she was dressed the way she was and she hoped he would stop staring. The man crumbled up the blue of his towel into a ball and tossed it on the ground and the twins watched it slowly unfold. Arnulfo and Ricky hopped across the seething, pocked pavement before the mother made good her promise.

—It's so hot, Ricky said.

—So tell us something we don't know, Estrella replied.

Petra led the string of heads with the children in the middle and Estrella at the end. They passed the red vending machine, and passed a woman wearing patent leather pumps who banged a fist against the machine until some quarters clanked to the slot below. Petra glanced at the woman's spiked heels. Was this like the woman who crossed Whittier Boulevard with Estrella's real father? The woman stared at Petra and then at the children and finally at Estrella who pointed to a coin near the woman's heel. Her skirt so tight, the woman stooped with difficulty and picked up the coin.

They passed the watchdog who lunged its purple belly wildly against a particular space on the lopping wire fence. The dog growled, his incisors showing from his purple lips, and barked until his bark grew into an angry howl.

—Shut up, Arnulfo ordered bravely from the other side of the fence. Shut that trap of yours!

—Good dog, nice dog, sweet dog, nice dog, Perla crooned, keeping her distance. The dog became quiet and pushed its black nose up against the wire mesh and the snotty slits of his nostrils flared open.

—I'll tell Mama, Cookie dared.

—He loves me, the twin Perla said.

—Don't go near ese perro loco! Petra yelled. Without warning, the dog opened its jaws wide and yawned and shook its snout, its collar rattling like keys, and sauntered his scruffy body to the supply shed where empty soda bottles nestled in metal crates.

—You scared him.

—Stay on the porch. ¡Y tú! Petra pointed at Ricky, Watcha las niñas.

Petra did not allow the children inside. The proprietor squinted whenever children flooded the store as if their touches dulled the value of his wares. And there were too many things to touch: pots and brooms and a barrel of pinto beans and tacked up posters of celebrities; slabs of fabric on the shelves and stacks of pirated cassette tapes. Cantinflas plaster of paris statues and canned goods and candles and propane lined up like soldiers. Too, the peppermint sticks were right at the children's eye level. This inspired such outlandish behavior that it made Petra spank them with a fierce, unjustified anger she later repented. A string of Christmas bells hung on the screen door with a rusty thumb tack though summer was here and the bells jingled as Petra pulled the door open.

—Buy me a raspada, Arnulfo pleaded.

—Stay in the shade of the porch, replied Petra.

—Don't let the flies out, Ricky said.

—Don't let the flies out! the proprietor said when he heard the clank and knock of the old bells. He chuckled as if his private joke never lost its punch, and he looked up from the ledger book as thick as a Bible and his nostrils grew wide and he pulled out his kerchief and swabbed his nose then poked the kerchief back into his vest pocket. The freezer in the back room of the store buzzed off and the store fell noticeably silent. The scent of burnt rubber hovered like the quiet.

—¡Puta madre! a voice said.

—¿Y qué gana hablando así!? Petra muttered to Estrella as she handed her a basket.

—You sure you can fix it? The proprietor yelled to the cursing voice in the back room. Yellowed and dusty crepe paper draped like sagging cable lines above the cash register.

—Trust me, the voice replied. A crank of motor buzzed on again and it reminded Petra how the bus engine sounded climbing the steep Interstate 5 mountain pass.

Petra picked up a can of El Pato Tomato sauce, checked the price, then checked a can of Carnation Milk, a jar of Tang, then returned each to the shelf. She decided on four cans of Spam and stacked them into Estrella's basket at $1.80 each for a seven-ounce can and made a mental calculation of $7.20, then returned the two cans and adjusted the amount, then realized the ESPECIAL that read three cans for $5.00 which meant to buy six cans was cheaper in the long run and placed four more cans in the basket.

The fresh produce was dumped into small zinc tubs and pushed against a wall and hardly resembled the crops harvested days before. The fruits and vegetables were firm and solid out in the hot fields; but here in the store, only the relics remained: squished old tomatoes spilled over onto the bruised apples and the jalapeños mixed with soft tomatillos and cucumbers peeked from between blotchy oranges. The white onions reminded Petra of eggs.

—We should get some eggs, Petra said, looking up at the posters tacked up on the wall behind the vegetable tubs. Except for the cans of Spam, the basket Estrella held was empty.

A lopsided poster of the holy Virgen, Our Lady of Guadalupe was tacked between the posters of Elvis Presley and Marilyn Monroe holding her white billowing dress down. La Virgen was adorned by red and green and white twinkling Christmas lights which surrounded the poster like a sequin necklace. Each time the lights blinked, Petra saw herself reflected in La Virgen's glossy downcast eyes. Unlike Marilyn's white pumps which were buried under the shrivelled pods of Chile Negro, La Virgen was raised, it seemed to Petra, above a heavenly mound of bulbous garlic.

—Can we? replied Estrella, You think we can get some eggs?

The freezer motor smelled of incense.

—We need to take garlic, Petra said. The top bulbs were obviously older: many had brown age spots or green sprouts. She plunged her arm deep into the pit of the tub knowing full well the fresher bulbs were at the bottom. Elbow deep, her hand felt for the firm hearty

110

bulbs while the top ones plummeted onto the floorboards like hail from the sky.

Her bare toes were blue against the gray garlic, and
for a moment, it looked like she stood amidst the
clouds. It was only by chance and the right angle of the
sunlight that she saw with her own eyes bulbous clouds
carrying her, until a big brown hand clamped a bunch
of bulbs and the hand brought her back. She followed
the hand up his wiry body so thin he needed a good
meal. His work pants were cuffed above his boots,
large cuffs deep enough to be pockets, and from under
the thick smell of incense, she saw a cap of baldness
rising to the surface. Moments passed between them
like years because it seemed like forever before she saw
his face.

Gray stubble lingered in the deep canyons of his
cheeks. He looked old, but the nature of their lives had
a way of putting twenty years on a face, so that a man
of fifty looked like he was seventy, and perhaps she
looked fifty herself, though she was only thirty-three at
the time.

He clamped another handful and raised it to his flattened nose and closed his eyes and inhaled with great
concentration. The glowing Christmas lights danced
against his bifocals. He opened his eyes and picked a
bulb from the bunch and held his selection up to her.
The smell was distinct, strong, but under its pungency
she detected the rosewater fragrance which made the
bulb particularly powerful. Petra turned to Estrella.

111

—See? You can smell it in this one, the roses, see, and you don't believe me! Look, she said, holding up the bulb, it's even blessed by La Virgen! but Estrella shrugged her shoulders not yet able to see the flower in the bulb. She placed it near the Spam.

—They never believe you, the man said.

—Gracias. Muy amable, Petra said after they finally cleared the floor of garlic. She extended her hand. He clasped it and his hand had the texture of tree bark and when he released her hand, she felt as if splinters had remained in her fingers.

His boots weighed loud on the floorboards for such a thin man. The red tool chest he carried seemed heavy; one shoulder dipped as he walked to the counter. He put his tool chest down and rested one shoe on the box.

—It had to do with the wires, the man said. He pulled some tangled wire threads from his pocket to explain but the proprietor dismissed the details with a wave of his kerchief and then tucked it into a cauliflower peeking from his pocket.

—Perfecto! the proprietor said in a shout. Your bill is paid up then.

—Can I have some ice?

—Of course, of course, the proprietor replied, slapping Perfecto's shoulder.

Petra split the bulging cloves of the clouds, smelled them, made sure their scent pricked her nose, felt the crinkly paper skin. These would be good crushed and boiled with milk for stomachache tonics, these would

112

be pickled with a little vinegar and stored in the shade and would ease the knots of her veins, and these had cloves big enough for dicing and adding to hot chile.

The man carried a burlap bag over his shoulder and the bag trickled down his back and to the floor and Petra smiled and he smiled back. With his free hand, his branch fingers clamped onto the metal handle of the tool chest, and Petra hurried to the door and pulled the screen door open and the Christmas bells drummed against the door like knuckles and the propietor said, —Don't let the flies out! and guffawed again.

Perfecto said, You're very kind, Miss, and he walked away, water dotting behind him.

The proprietor breathed through his mouth, his breathing loud and dry. He snapped two bags open and placed the cans of Spam at the bottom, and garlic and onions at the top. Petra wondered why he bothered with a mustache at all; his bigotes were so thin, it looked as straight as the dash he penciled after every credit.

—Making garlic soup? He asked in a tone which, if one were cynical, could be taken as sarcasm.

—I'll sell you a pot, Petra replied.

—For some eggs, Estrella added.

—I don't have any, he said.

—I didn't think so, Petra said, handing a bag to Estrella.

The proprietor opened the ledger to a page darkened at the right-hand corner by the moist tips of his finger and turned it around for Petra to sign. The freezer buzzed off and the two followed the drops of water out.

—Whatta you got in your mouth? Petra raised Cookie's chin, inspecting her daughter's face suspiciously. The twin sat on the porch crunching. What are you eating?

—Ice, Ricky replied, a jagged piece melting from between his fingers, A nice man, he gave us ice. He chewed like a chipmunk. The melting ice streaked down his hand and dribbled to the porch step.

—What man? asked Petra glancing, but all Ricky did was point towards the vacant highway.

—It was gave to us, Cookie said. Her cheeks glowed red like a fever. She crunched the last of hers and stared at Ricky's piece.

Petra placed the paper sack down, then picked the bag up, crumbling the top of the bag so tight it sounded like fire. She looked down the long stretch of the road again. Trust me, he had said when she entered the store, and by chance, she would. The highway seemed endless and hot and dry and wet all at the same time: asphalt held down the heat of the day's sun like her heart did with hope. Ice, what was in a piece of ice?

—Vámonos, Petra said.

The watchdog growled when they passed, and Petra kicked the fence and the fence wobbled and the dog retreated, then clawed an itch with a hind leg, his purple testicles shaking like coin purses. The twin Perla spit a piece of ice on the palm of her hand and flung it over the wire fence. The dog rolled his pink tongue on the ice.

—Remember me, she instructed the dog, I love you.

Petra stared at the day-blue sheet that divided the two rooms in the bungalow. The sheet was thinner than a minute and swayed with a hint of cool morning breeze. There was no light except for the expanding dawn and the sheet against the darkened morning fluttered like Perfecto's whistling lips. He lay on his back, one arm bent over his head as if he were about to throw something, thin stray hairs in the valley of his armpit. He snored, loose skin collapsing around his Adam's apple. Perfecto mumbled in his sleep, then turned his back to her, taking most of the quilt. His neck and shoulders had a permanent sunburn, so even though his back was bare, his belly as white and soft as cream, it seemed as if he still wore a T-shirt. She pulled at the quilt to regain a portion.

Petra rubbed the heat of her stomach. To deny her body would be to deny the morning now rising, would be as useless as pressing her palms against her ears to silence the chattering of the birds who awakened at the first light of day. She heard Perfecto's deep guttural snore. He was the only man she knew who made more noise in his sleep than in his waking hours. Then she heard them talking. Like the birds, they, too, awoke with the first light.

—Star?

115

—Yeah?

—Pass me some water.

—Feel better?

—Yeah. Thanks.

—A lot of us are getting it. Mama's been throwing up a lot too.

Petra heard this. She pulled the quilt and squeezed her breasts against Perfecto's back, felt her heart pounding between them.

—And you?

—I'm okay. But I don't want Ricky and Arnulfo out there. They can't know how to work with the sun yet.

—Like me?

—Meaning like you or not like you?

—You're making my head hurt.

—Your bruise looks better.

—Do you think I'm handsome?

—I better get up.

—Wait, wait. I wish I could spend a whole day with you and talk about everything under the sky. I mean it.

To Petra, Alejo's voice seemed deeper now than when he first came. Perfecto murmured a response to something asked in his dream. She could not tell what he whispered and she wondered if it was another nightmare.

—Did you have any dreams? Petra heard Estrella ask. She saw her daughter's words come to her. She could swear the words forced the corner of the sheet up

116

and obediently floated like a streamer to her. She loved her daughter very much.

—I'll remember by tonight. It was strange though, like I was falling or something. And you?

—I don't have dreams.

—Everyone does, you just don't remember.

—That's not true.

—Let me hold you.

Petra heard the shifting of bodies. Was Estrella squeezing against Alejo, as she was doing with Perfecto? Petra stared at the sheet. How blind could she have been? Hadn't she learned something in her thirty-five years? Is this what it was all about, healing Alejo so that he could take Estrella? She urged her hips against Perfecto's buttocks, then ran her arm under his and let it rest over the breadth of his belly. She felt as if she held nothing, his body like a phantom of a man once made of hearty flesh. She was amazed at the thickness of his ribs, though his skin was tissue loose and soft. She flipped her leg over his hip.

—What grade are you in?

—I don't know.

—You always gonna work in the fields?

What a stupid boy! Petra thought, her nose pressed against Perfecto's neck. She smelled traces of Dixie peach pomade on his hair and the scent made her nauseous. What right did he have to ask that? If Estrella wasn't working, there would be nothing for him to eat.

—What's wrong with picking the vegetables people'll be eating for dinner?

—But you always wanna do it?

—I sure hope not.

Petra felt Perfecto touch her hand with his big parchment fingers and she found his gesture tender. Love, Petra knew, came and went. But it was loyalty that kept them on the tightrope together when it was gone, kept them from seeing the void beneath their feet and yes she had learned something in her thirty-five years. Hadn't she learned that love would return if she were patient enough? Just keep your balance, tiptoe across the tightrope, one foot up one foot down, don't look below. And wait. She felt Perfecto grab her hand if only for a moment, then push it away, in a gesture that was not mean, just definite.

—Let me hold you. Petra heard the young man Alejo whisper to her daughter. She finally sat up and punched her fists through a T-shirt, then through her sweater sleeves. Her feet slipped into her rubber sandals. She pulled her skirt up over her nylon slip and she tried twice to clamp the waist with a safety pin, but it pressed too tight against her belly. She opened the door to the morning, the door creaking in its hinges, and a sharp slap of breeze stung her cheek. As she stood on the porch, the gray morning filtered through the black trees and they reminded her of papel picado. She sighed, a deep exhale of cool air. Each morning she held nothing back. But the day bloomed and time became a tight squeeze of a belt upon a belly. Petra forced herself down the steps. Hadn't she learned anything in her thirty-five years? That her two hands couldn't hold anything back, including time?

When it perched on the branch to rest, the crow eyed the woman's head near the smoking fire. The wind disturbed the branch under its claws and the bird glided downward. It pecked on the stable ground not far from the smoke.

Three fingers of Clabber Girl baking powder, sprinkle of salt (a little salt over the left shoulder for luck), a few handfuls of La Pina flour, Rex lard, and warm water from the aluminum coffeepot. Knead. Let the white mound stand with a dishcloth over it. Boil. Put the coffee grinds in the pot. Sauté the papas with diced onion and tomato and lard. Remove the dishcloth, begin rolling the tortillas.

Petra stopped to look at the bird which pumped its wide wings upward, a twig in its beak. The smell of woodsmoke brought Petra back to her place and she took another small mound of kneaded dough, dusted it with flour and began to roll it on an oval cutting board. She did this like awakening without a clock, like taking a drink when she was thirsty, sometimes singing under her breath, sometimes thinking about too many things at once.

Starting in the middle, she rolled from north to south, flipped the dough, sprinkled flour, turned to remove the tortilla already baking on the comal, returned to roll from east to west until the tortilla was perfectly round, then place it on the comal, get more dough, sprinkled flour, turned to remove the baked tortilla from the comal and stack it on top of the others. Spoon the potatoes in the flour tortilla so nothing would spill. Fold the bottom of the tortilla, then the top, then the sides so that the burrito was a perfect envelope, then rewrap the burritos in foil for the lunches. She could do this in the dark, ill or healthy, near some trees, by a road, on a door made into a table or while birds flew past her with twigs between their beaks because tortillas filled her children's stomachs and made their stomachs hungry for more.

Her eldest daughter emerged from the bungalow barefooted, carrying her shoes in one hand, socks in the other, walking gingerly on the splintering floor planks of the porch. How tall she had gotten within a matter of months. Estrella would be fourteen soon. Soon? Soon Estrella would begin menstruation, and Petra thought of blood in the glow of the fire, the amber red of molten wood, and in the absence of her own menstruation. Was she waiting as well?

When she was Estrella's age, Petra feared many things. Crooked backs, cancer, evil eye. Petra took a clove of garlic and ground it in the molcajete, and then added another when she thought of bewitchment. The first time she saw her own undergarment darkened with

purple blood, she swore she was bleeding to death because no one had told her otherwise. The crow flew
away with another and longer twig between its beak
and Petra studied its flight until it disappeared among
the eucalyptus. When it was time, it was time and not
even Petra's glare at her eldest daughter was enough to
halt the weather of what was to come, halt the flesh
and blood pieces of Estrella's heart from falling to the
ground. Petra ground deeper into the garlic.

Estrella crisscrossed her shoelaces over her trouser
cuffs while the mother flipped a tortilla. Sweet Jesus
how she wished it would rain and they wouldn't have
to go to the fields today. The mother poured coffee in
a blue enamel cup, stirred in three heaping teaspoons
of sugar from a Yuban coffee can, blew into it. The
tortilla baking on top of the black cast-iron comal, the
cawing of crows, the mother stirring sugar in the black
coffee. This morning was no different. What would it
take to get out of the fields? Her pants were stiff with
dirt and felt scratchy against her legs. The day hadn't
even begun and already she felt tired.

The creak of Perfecto Flores' boots passed her without a word and he stepped down to where the mother
delivered his cup of coffee. Estrella knew he would re-
main silent until she agreed to help tear down the barn.
She rolled her head, her neck stiff, stood to stretch,
rubbed the palm of her hand. Tomorrow was Sunday.
She yawned, not wanting to move, but the scent of fried

121

papas, red chile with crushed garlic boiling on the grate, and steaming coffee enticed her to the table where Perfecto sipped his coffee loudly. He sat on a crate, one hand flattened on his knee, his bifocals fogging from the steam of the hot coffee when he brought it to his lips.

—You and Alejo are like birds that make too much noise, the mother said between rolls of the pin. Estrella knew Perfecto was angry but never counted on the mother being angry as well.

—He likes to talk, Mama.

—Well? This from Perfecto. Can I count on you?

—Count on her for what? Petra asked.

—What do you want me to say, Perfecto Flores?

—¿Y tú, tú qué quieres? The mother said, pointing the rolling pin to her, then giving Estrella her back.

—¿Yo? Mama. No más comida. Es todo. Estrella held a cup of coffee but hadn't realized she had poured herself one.

—And the next thing is . . . the mother continued her rolling . . . and the next thing is that's how it all starts.

—You going crazy again, Petra? Perfecto replied, tossing the rest of the coffee out, a black blot like fingers on the ground near the crows. They raised their wings in a threat of flight, but instead moved farther away and continued their pecking.

—How you feeling, Mama?

—Así comienza todo. The mother flipped a tortilla. That's how it all starts. She singed her finger on the hot comal, and cried out so loud, the crows flew away a few more yards from the table.

Petra guided Alejo to the porch and propped him on the crate. She was weary of battling sickness. His cheeks were sunken, pale, and she thought the sun might pull some blood into his skin. He leaned his head back and rested and looked at her in a way that she no longer recognized. She pressed a penny to his forehead not far from where his bruise had healed, until the penny engraved a red ring in his skin when she removed it. She studied the color of the ring, placed the penny in her pocket. Some days were better than others, but still he was too weak to work, too weak to stand, and only perked up, rinsed his mouth, rubbed the mucus from the corners of his eyes, when Estrella returned to the bungalow.

The twins played not far from the porch, disrupting the flow of red ants. They followed the ants with dirt, delighted to see the ants dig themselves out of the pile they poured on top of them. Perla and Cookie scooped more dirt and let it slip between their fingers and giggled.

Petra went back to cleaning nopales. She stripped away the spines of the beaver tail cactus with her butcher knife over a piece of paper bag torn open. How long could they afford to take care of him? The gummy sap of the nopal was making her own mouth salivate. She had tried everything to cure him. The egg for nausea, the glass of water placed above his head for sunstroke, espigas de maíz with sulfur matches, ground to an ash and mixed with boiled water for an elixir. But some days were better than others.

Petra took care of Alejo, not because of who he was, but because she was a mother too, and if Estrella was sick, or Ricky and Arnulfo were sick in the piscas, she would want someone to take care of them. And of course, she did it for the love of God. This, however, was more than she had anticipated, and she just didn't have the strength. Her legs were swelling with varicose veins which ruptured like earthquake fault lines. Remembering Perfecto's withdrawal, she wondered if he thought she had failed somehow.

Gums of spit rolled in her mouth and she pressed the corner of her apron to her lips. Petra ambled to the side of the house, her sandals clicking. Cookie and Perla looked up from the ant hole. She leaned a hand against the wall, heaved the breakfast that stuck like pasty glue until it finally erupted, scorching her throat and flying out of her mouth. The flies immediately began to buzz around her, and she kicked some dirt over the vomit. She would pray tonight, burn incense made of mustard seeds and corn and cachana. She had failed, failed the test. Petra went back to cleaning nopales. Not even

sucking on a lemon wedge could eliminate the lingering
bitterness in her mouth.

Estrella slept with her now. They slept like two
hands pressed together in prayer. Under the roof of the
bungalow, Petra thought of the lima bean in her, the
bean floating in the night of her belly, bursting a root
with each breath. Would the child be born without a
mouth, would the poisons of the fields harden in its tiny
little veins?

And the night became morning again and Estrella
would awake counting the ticking of her own heart.
The mother slept so close to her, Estrella could feel her
breath suck in long warm streams of her air like a cat
who steals away the breaths of a newborn.

—Perfecto, what are we gonna do? Estrella asked.
She poured water in a bowl, cupped her hand and wet
the brick limestone. She took hold of her crescent moon
knife, pressed a palm on the sliver of steel and scraped
long against the limestone until her knife glittered sharp
in the lantern light.

Perfecto turned a bucket upside down and sat near
the smoldering pit. He propped his bare foot on one
knee. A Coca-Cola bottle boiled in a steel pot of water,
and bounced like an egg. He sliced off the dry, white
calluses of his heel with a buck knife leaving a tender
boil on his foot exposed. He looked up to see Estrella

rubbing the curve of her knife with a dishtowel. Moths fluttered around the lantern.

—Three weeks work with the two of us working, Perfecto replied, pushing his bifocals up the bridge of his nose with the back of his hand. The mother prayed in the house, her knees like puddles in the dark while the children slept. We can even resell the cedar shakes from the roof and keep the money.

A bonfire in the distant camp scraped the dark, the sparks of cinders rising. She tossed the dirty water out, placed the knife in her basket and lowered the kerosene of the lantern.

—Is the bottle ready? He asked, holding his toes. Estrella held the lantern up and leaned over the pit. She nodded, then placed the lantern down, and grabbed two rags and took hold of the boiling pot. She took it over to Perfecto.

—Alejo needs a doctor. She said, hoping he would understand and accept the barter.

—I thought it was your mama . . . I thought she'd be the one, Perfecto replied, taken aback. Estrella's face had a strange yellowish glow over the burning lantern light.

—Is she sicker, Perfecto?

—I'm not a doctor and neither are you.

—He can't talk anymore. He loved to talk, Perfecto, don't you see?

—And your mama?

—Why are you making me choose?

126

—Because it comes down to that.

—She knows.

—She knows what? Hand me those pliers, Perfecto said with authority. He pushed his bifocals up again. She handed him the long-nosed pliers, and they trembled in his hand as he plucked the bottle and shook out the remaining hot water. He held it near the fire to dry it off.

—We need the money. We need to tear the barn down before the Foreman gives the job to someone else, Estrella said.

Perfecto wrapped a rag around the base of the thick-glassed bottle. Now sterilized, he took the mouth of the bottle and pressed it over the boil.

—Puta madre, he grunted, as if the two words incanted painkillers. He winced as the boil erupted, white and green and blood pus gushing into the bottle.

—You should have let Mama do that.

—I'm old enough, he replied, wincing again. I can take care of myself.

With the same rag she used to take the pot off the fire, Estrella pressed the tender sole of his foot. He pushed the bottle into the fire, and the wood sparked and cinders rose and the bottle blackened with soot immediately.

—Puta madre. The tire spun endlessly in the mud. Perfecto stood near the rear of the station wagon to watch. They were headed to the medical clinic, the muffler loud and vibrating on the unpaved road. A broken water pipe bubbled up and muddied a section of the road that Perfecto didn't notice until the wagon's back tire dipped and sunk into the deep chocolate mud. He raised his finger for Petra to gas it. Perfecto on his haunches now, studied the tire spinning. ¡Puta madre!

—¿Y qué ganas hablando así? asked Petra through the driver side window. Petra punched the gas pedal again. The tire was buried up to the axle in mud and it spun like a treadmill. One by one the doors of the station wagon opened and they all stepped out except for Alejo. He lay on the worn carpet, wrapped in a cotton blanket in the back, above the trunk of tools and spare tire. It had happened before. The tire getting stuck in mud or sand was not new.

Except for the twins, who stood by the side of the road, the others pushed against the chrome dented bumper of the station wagon. Uno dos tres. Petra gunned the motor. Uno dos tres. When the wagon did not move, the children got to working: the boys collected piles of rocks, the girls twigs and branches. Perfecto opened the hatchback of the wagon. He did not want to disturb Alejo who could barely lift his chin up. But, in order to get the spade shovel, he had to slide Alejo's feet over and pull open the door to the hidden trunk where a crumpled paper bag was shoved behind the red painted jack and crowbar. In order to do that, he had to lift Alejo's callused sweaty feet. The way Alejo's big toes inverted from ill-fitting shoes disturbed him. He removed the bag, closed the trapdoor, slid Alejo's feet to their original position. Inside the bag were jumper cables, flashlight, oval of wire for the muffler, a roll of toilet paper, screwdrivers, a small-head hammer, and the garden spade shovel. He took the shovel, nervously rumpled the bag, and then banged the wagon door shut with unusual force.

Perfecto dug around the tire with the shovel, sweat causing his bifocals to slip down his nose, shaky from attempting to push the car.

—Perfecto Flores, Estrella said, tapping the top of his straw hat gently, Let me do it. You get behind the wheel. Without objecting, he relinquished the shovel and leaned against the hood of the wagon, struggling for breath. Petra began to unbutton the collar of his shirt, but Perfecto pushed her hand away from his throat.

The mud came up to the calves of her legs and she felt as if there wasn't any solid earth to ground herself. Estrella dug and scooped and clawed the muddy soil around the tire until the hole was deep enough to pave with rocks. She thought of the young girl that Alejo had told her about, the one girl they found in the La Brea Tar Pits. They found her in a few bones. No details of her life were left behind, no piece of cloth, no ring, no doll. A few bits of bone displayed somewhere under a glass case and nothing else.

Estrella's shoes were completely buried in the mud. She lined the rocks as she had seen Perfecto do before,

129

embedding them like a cobblestone road, and then snapped the twigs in two, propped the sticks over the various sized stones to give the tire traction to barrel out. It took an hour to complete. Her hands were caked with gray dried mud, and although it was not the thing to do, she wiped her hands against her dress, then shook off the loose dirt. Estrella gave the signal and Perfecto revved the motor.

They stood by the side of the road and waited. Perfecto gunned the motor and the tire spun. Arnulfo crossed his fingers. The twins covered their ears. Alejo lifted his head up and looked through the splattered rear window while Petra held her breath because the black fumes of exhaust made her nauseous. But the tire only spun deeper into the hole, the rocks and twigs spitting from beneath, all of them watching as the tire spun and spun without moving an inch.

Four

Four

*T*he white trailer stuck out like partially buried bone in the middle of the vacant plot. The compact square windows facing the highway had foil taped to the framed sliding glass which deflected the sun. A small porch awning was held up by two hollow poles planted solidly in Folgers coffee cans filled with dried cement. Perfecto turned into the graveled drive. The gravel crushed and spit and the muffler trembled and Estrella leaned forward from the backseat, her head between the mother and Perfecto Flores to see the gas gauge bury the E, and Perfecto flicked a fingernail a few times to make sure the gauge wasn't stuck. Perfecto parked between an orange and white ambulance, its rusty chassis propped up with mason bricks and a black Rambler with a white top. The tires of the ambulance were missing and Estrella sat back to think.

The station wagon knocked and pinged even after Perfecto removed the key from the ignition. He sat quietly in front of the white trailer, as if the mud and the tire and Alejo and Petra had squeezed his heart out and his tired bones wanted to sit behind the steering wheel for a moment, real quiet. He rubbed his eyes under his bifocals, waited for someone to do something. He had done his part. He got them there. The heat in the car immediately began to rise.

—¿Amá? Estrella asked. But the mother sat quietly, Perfecto's straw hat on her lap. Estrella opened her door, and the rest followed.

They had been stuck on the road most of the afternoon, repaving, digging deeper into the soil to get the wagon out of the mud. Finally, by late afternoon, the mud had dried somewhat and the roadside dust rose as a truckload of piscadores returned to the camp in a blue pickup, its rattling panel wood boards jostling the men who rested their heads against its rhythm. The twins waved and cheered, and the piscadores jumped off the pickup to help. The driver moved closer to the wagon's rear bumper while a few of the men stood like pallbearers on either side of the wagon. They briefly glanced at Alejo wrapped in his blanket, one of them even tapping the window with a scraped knuckle, but once they saw him, they averted their glances, steadied their boots, determined not to look again. Uno dos tres, púshale.

Finally, by late afternoon, the wagon was freed to their relief. Perfecto shook hands. With one hand he pumped his gratitude while his other hand lightly slapped their shoulders, the dust rising, the men smiling. Petra crossed herself in gratitude then said thank you over and over like a string of repetitive prayers.

All this, just to arrive at a heap of aluminum foil and missing tires.

Perfecto held the pole of the awning. The cement was loose, the pole wobbly. He noted it.

The clinic smelled of strong disinfectant and bad plumbing. There were three folding chairs opposite the entrance. Estrella helped Alejo to one of them and his weight released a breath on the chair. Only the hum of a fan could be heard. The mother remarked that nobody was present and perhaps the clinic was closed, but Estrella replied the fan was still on and the door unlocked and the Rambler parked outside which meant that the clinic was open and Perfecto agreed with both of them. Above the chair was a poster of two frisky kittens romping. Alejo leaned his head back against the ball of yarn the kittens played with and closed his eyes.

The place was empty, but the fan in the corner continued to rotate, blowing a triangle of air in the room. A curtain rod needled in and out of a yellow cloth hanging limp at a window behind a desk which fluttered only momentarily when the air of the fan blasted it. Ricky peeked behind the curtain as the fan moved to another corner, then returned to blast him with warm air.

Perfecto slid his hand on the wood-panel wall, checked for a loose knob. He read the room for signs of disrepair so that he could barter his services for theirs. He knew by instinct, and he thought of a shellac paint job as he ran his big flattened palm against the flaking wood grain. The smell of bad plumbing. A toilet needing repairing, what else?

To the side of the desk were woodpressed counters which the twins immediately inspected. They tiptoed to reach eye level above the counter. There was a row of glass jars filled with flat tongue depressors that reminded them of fat ice cream sticks, gauze pads and cotton swabs on skinny wooden sticks that looked like the legs of ballet dancers in tan nylons and white shoes; thermometers in a glass tube and a big jar of cotton balls. Cookie picked up a rubber mallet that lay on a silver tray and Perla tattled on her.

The cotton balls in the jar looked too white, like imitation cotton to Petra. She noticed a scale near the desk much like the one used for measuring the weight of picked cotton. The scale reminded her how she'd wet the cotton or hid handsized rocks in the middle of her sack so that the scale tipped in her favor when the cotton was weighed. The scale predicted what she would be able to eat, the measurement of her work and the

136

thought that she had to cheat for food made her resentful of any scale, including this one.

Perfecto removed his glasses and it was only then that he caught sight of his face in the silver towel dispenser and realized how dirty his face was because the space where his glasses had once been made him look as if he still wore goggles. He pulled a towel out, ran it under the tap, and wiped his face. He rubbed his eyes and his eyes watered and put his glasses back on to see himself. Old, so old.

Then they heard the jingling of keys.

A young woman emerged holding her purse and car keys. She looked both surprised and distraught. She had on a fresh coat of red lipstick, and the thick scent of carnation perfume made Estrella think she was there in the trailer all along, in the bathroom. The woman looked at her Timex wristwatch.

—What have we here?

—He's real sick. Estrella pointed to Alejo. She became aware of her own appearance. Dirty face, fingernails lined with mud, her tennis shoes soiled, brown smears like coffee stains on her dress where she had cleaned her hands. The nurse's white uniform and red lipstick and flood of carnations made her even more self-conscious. It amazed Estrella that some people never seemed to perspire while others like herself sweated gallons.

—Some people have all the luck, the nurse said, going to her desk. She checked her watch once more and paused for a moment. She took hold of the key and unlocked a bottom drawer and she slipped her purse in and closed it and opened a top drawer. She pulled out the stethoscope and placed it in her pocket. She sat down on a squeaking chair and ripped a fresh sheet of paper out of a tablet. From her pencil cup, next to the photographs of two smiling boys, she lifted a pen.

—He was named after his grandfather on his father's side.

—Yes, but his last name.

—Hidalgo, like in Hidalgo County, Texas, Estrella lied.

—Is he a relative?

—¿Qué dice? asked Petra. To her, this clinic business was a racket. She felt uncomfortable and wished she had on her duck apron with the big pockets where she could hide her hands.

—She wants to know if he's related to us. I think we should say yes.

—Claro, replied the mother. Tell her he's my nephew.

—He's her nephew.

—And this must be grandpa.

—He's her husband, Estrella lied a second time.

—How long has Alex-hoes been sick?

—A few months.

—Just when I think it can't get any hotter . . . The nurse picked up the paper she had penciled, and fanned herself with it. The mother whispered a question to Estrella.

—How much will the doctor be? asked Estrella.

—What you see is what you get. The nurse flipped the calendar pages through the silver hoops above the desk blotter and checked dates. Dr. Martínez isn't coming for another week. Now let's take care of this sweet thing. Can you stand on the scale for me, can you ask him if he could stand on the scale for me?

—He's the spelling bee champ of Hidalgo County. He understands English.

Petra imagined there were rocks in Alejo's pockets. He dragged his bare feet as if the remaining flesh on his bones was too heavy and she couldn't help but think of rocks in the cotton sacks of his bones, his eyes and stomach, his pockets, rocks.

Estrella helped Alejo. There was something unsettling about this whole affair to Estrella, but she couldn't stop long enough to figure out what it was. Alejo's arm hooked over her neck and she almost had to drag him to the scale. She stumbled, slowed her pace even more. She felt like crying, an ache in her chest, just as she had felt a while back when she tried paving the rocks so carefully, worked so hard. But the tire resisted, Alejo's body resisted, and she did not want to think what she was thinking now: God was mean and did not care and she was alone to fend for herself. She dragged Alejo's weight against her, his hot breath on her cheek, his ribs like barren branches trembling in a winter night. All she wanted was to find a deep, dark quiet place like the barn to cry. That was due her. She deserved it. Things would get better after that, because they couldn't get any worse.

The nurse moved the weights on the scale, jotted it down on the paper, pointed her pencil to the examination table, then slipped the pencil behind her ear. She helped Estrella with Alejo while Perfecto and Petra watched nervously from the sidelines, not wanting to transgress the medical protocol of the clinic.

The paper crumpled as Alejo lay down on the examination table. Estrella didn't want him to feel like a slab of beef on butcher paper and so she ran the back of her knuckles against his cheek and he managed a smile until the nurse shooed her away. Estrella stood near the wall where the blood pressure machine was mounted.

—Why didn't you bring him sooner? the nurse asked as she wrapped the Velcro cloth around his arm. Does your mama's husband speak English? The question threw Estrella off and she remained silent.

—He doesn't, whispered Alejo. His voice was reedy, cracking like dry mud. Then he felt as if someone had slugged him in the belly and he cradled himself.

—In that case, can we get everybody to the chairs except for this gal here.

—I don't want her to see me. Alejo wanted to be left alone, but Estrella stood by anyway.

Estrella watched the silver mercury pump up the barometer, and the metallic liquid was beautiful, like a moon riding on a geyser, like an upside down waterfall. The mercury jumped once, lowered, jumped again, a third time, then rushed down to a pool at the bottom. Pulsating. Metallic and fluid. Solid and diffused. The nurse removed the plugs of her stethoscope, jotted something on the paper.

Petra did not like all this jotting and poking the nurse was doing. She had smelled the carnations even before the nurse appeared and the smell repulsed her and she fought against upchucking right there into the shiny trash barrel. The nurse should know better than to wear something so venomous to pregnant women as carnations. Even the many things on the nurse's desk implied fakery; the pictures of her smiling boys (Who did they think they were, smiling so boldly at the camera?), the porcelain statue of a calico kitten with a little stethoscope, wearing a folded white cap with a red cross between its too cute perky little ears; a pile of manila folder files stacked in a strange way that seemed cluttered and disordered. She wore too much red lipstick, too much perfume and asked too many questions and seemed too clean, too white just like the imitation cotton. She may fool other people but certainly not her. Enough. Get the young man well enough so that he could return to Edinburg. As she saw Estrella touch Alejo's cheek, she wondered for the first time about contagious ailments.

—Don't you worry, she'll be behind this curtain, just

keeping us company. Estrella heard the Velcro rip of the blood pressure wrap, the rattle of shower curtain rings when the nurse pulled the curtain between she and Alejo.

—How much is all this gonna cost? asked Petra, spitting into the trash can, but no one answered.

—I think the boy's got dysentery. But I'm not a doctor, and I got no lab for sampling. You gonna have to get him to the main hospital in Corazón. He's got all the signs of dehydration.

—¿Qué dice del corazón? asked the mother.

—Sweet Jesus, Estrella said. We gotta take him to the hospital in Corazón.

—¿Esta loca la enfermera?

—Amá, Alejo's sicker then we thought.

—He's not our responsibility. This from Perfecto Flores.

—Es la verdad. Su primo Gumecindo lo puede llevar al hospital. Vámonos, Perfecto.

—You know he's gone back. The mother shrugged her shoulders. I can't believe you, Mama.

—Piénsalo, hija. Does he have papers? What if the hospital reports him.

—He was born in Texas. His grandma was born there too and her grandma. They belong here, Mama.

—Does he have money? You got money? Whose gonna pay?

—Perfecto Flores, what do we do?

Perfecto rubbed the baldness of his head. Why wasn't he wearing his hat? Damn if he couldn't remember if he left it in the car or in the house.

—Is Alejo gonna die? asked Perla.

—Shut up!

—Ricky, take the twins to the shade over there. Now.

—But . . .

—You heard your mother, unless you want a nalgazo!

—Why can't Arnulfo take the twins?

—Why don't we ask Alejo what he wants. Estrella bit a hangnail.

—I know what he wants.

—You gave your word, Perfecto.

—Puta madre. ¿Dónde está Corazón?

The fan seemed feeble against the heat which was more intense inside the trailer. Alejo's shirt was unbuttoned, and from his belly button, a straight, thin line of black hair sprouted to his chest. Estrella saw his nipples like two pennies and his body had colors that she had never noticed before. His belly was as white as hominy, veins of tarnished blue under his tongue, the gold of ears, the half moon of fingernails, his palms like the morning light. His hand, the one she held, was the color of sweet piloncillo. And Estrella couldn't hold the wind of his life as easily as she held his clammy hand. The nurse went over to her desk and sat and wrote on the

143

manila folder until she looked up to rearrange the picture frames of her smiling sons as if someone had disturbed their original position.

—The clinic visit is fifteen dollars, but I'll charge you only ten because . . . she paused and glanced at Estrella, then added, because I know times are hard these days. She removed her black patent leather purse from the bottom drawer and placed it on the desk beside the phone. Estrella stared at the nurse an extra second. How easily she put herself in a position to judge.

Estrella spread open both her hands and held them up for Perfecto to see. Petra saw her do this, and it made her think of when people surrender to the police or La Migra and how they put their hands up when they see the pistols pointed at the bull's-eye of their bellies. Petra was outraged.

—¡Diez dólares! ¿Y por qué diez? No más para decir que está enfermo el joven. Por gratis yo le digo la misma cosa. ¡Qué racketa!

Perfecto slipped his battered leather wallet from out of his back pocket. The wallet was shaped like the contours of his hip, round corners, thin, and contained an expired driver's license, his green card, a photo of a child of an acquaintance he no longer remembered, and strips of paper, receipts for reimbursements or reminders of money owed. He slipped out a five, then one dollar, two, three. And that was that. A deep darkened mouth gaped between the lips of the wallet. He checked a second time, looked up at Estrella. He dug into his pockets deep for coins, counted the assorted change. Altogether, change and bills, the total came to $9.07. Perfecto asked Estrella to ask the nurse if the toilet needed fixing. He would do this, and sand and paint this wall, for services rendered.

—He wants to know, Estrella said, flipping her thumb over her shoulder at Perfecto. He wants to know if he could maybe fix your toilet. He's very good, she added, His name's Perfecto because . . .

—Not to worry. The nurse waved her off, unlocked a tin money box, and removed a receipt book from inside. Listen, a few pennies short don't mean much.

—This is all we have, I think . . .

—The toilet don't need fixing. It's the heat is all.

—Tell her.

—He says . . .

—The poles.

—The poles outside . . .

—Need to be recemented.

—The poles outside need new cement. Maybe can he do that instead of the money?

—I only work here. I'm real sorry, the nurse replied, I couldn't say.

Estrella explained to Perfecto who was still hesitant about giving up the money. In the end, he gave it to her, placing the coins on top as if the thinly worn bills were a raft. She handed it to the nurse and the nurse placed a purple carbon between two sheets of the receipt book and pressed hard, misspelling the name.

When she was done, she separated the pennies from the dimes and nickels, counted the money and slid it into her palm and placed the bills and coins in the appropriate slots of the tin box and the coins dropping sounded like uncooked pinto beans dropping into a steel pot. The nurse closed the box, locked it, placed it in the top drawer, and handed the receipt to Estrella who handed it to Perfecto who stared at it, then placed it in his wallet where the money had once been and the mother folded her arms above her bosom.

—You're gonna get sicker if you don't get to a hospital. It's your call, Estrella whispered, helping Alejo do up his shirt like a mother buttoning a child against the cold.

—Take me home, Alejo replied faintly. His tongue was caked white and swollen and his hot breath on her face smelled sour.

—Where?

—Back home. Alejo closed his eyes.

—Come on, Alejo, don't do this to me. What do you mean?

—Hon, you gotta understand. I gotta pick up my kids in Daisyfield by six. The nurse checked her watch a third time, a pile of keys in her hand.

—How far is the hospital?

—A stone's throw away. About twenty miles, 281 East. Corazón turnoff. The nurse pointed.

—Perfecto can clear the high weeds around the door,

maybe plant some seedlings. What do you say? Estrella remembered the pictures of boys in framed smiles. Maybe I can baby-sit? Come on . . .

—I'm gonna have to lock up real soon.

—We're gonna have to go. . . . Estrella glanced around the room. She knew that they couldn't leave, but knew, too, the nurse was being stubborn. She would do anything at this point, Perfecto as well, the mother too. But they couldn't leave, they couldn't go. They had no money except for what Perfecto relinquished to pay for what the mother said they already knew, which seemed to her unfair.

Estrella thought for a moment as the heat condensed into sweat which trickled between her breasts in the trailer room when the nurse clicked off the fan. She tried to make her mind work, tried to imagine them back on the road with an empty gas tank and wallet and Alejo too sick to talk. She stared at Perfecto's tired face. The wrinkles on his face etched deeper with the sweat and soil and jagged sun. Was this the same panic the mother went through? There was no bartering this time. If only the nurse would consent. Estrella knew she couldn't get him home, but the hospital was only twenty miles. A simple nod, a break. If only God could help.

Estrella stared at the mother's resentfulness, at whom, what, she didn't know. They were not asking for charity, not begging for money. She stared at Alejo's forehead. All that was left of his fall was a darkened scar. They would all work, including the boys if they had to, to pay for the visit, to pay for gas. Alejo was sick and the nine dollars was gas money.

She remembered the tar pits. Energy money, the fossilized bones of energy matter. How bones made oil and oil made gasoline. The oil was made from their bones, and it was their bones that kept the nurse's car from not halting on some highway, kept her on her way to Daisyfield to pick up her boys at six. It was their bones that kept the air conditioning in the cars humming, that kept them moving on the long dotted line on the map. Their bones. Why couldn't the nurse see that? Estrella had figured it out: the nurse owed *them* as much as they owed her.

—Maybe, Estrella asked again, but this time the nurse didn't even look up as she filed the folder away.

Estrella walked out the door and out to the car. She didn't know what she was about to do, but had to do something to get the money for the gas for the hospital for Alejo. The doors of the wagon were unlocked and the twins, and Ricky and Arnulfo were playing under the shade of the oak tree, making circles with pebbles they had collected. They looked up only for a moment as Estrella opened the back door, pulled open the hidden trunk door, grabbed the crowbar which laid next to the red jack, heavy, iron cold, and walked back to the clinic. Perfecto was already walking out with Alejo, the mother behind them, but they froze as she approached. They moved aside to let Estrella pass, then U-turned and followed her. Perfecto laid Alejo on the vacant chairs.

When she reentered the clinic, the fan was off and the air was still and as thick as muck against her body. There was no turning back. But Estrella moved forward to the desk, the crowbar locked in her two fists.

—Give us back our money. Her heart dripped sweat. She felt the sweat puddle and dampen the soles of her feet. When the nurse looked up, it was only then that Estrella noticed how perfect her lipstick was.

—What are you talking about? The nurse, who now held her black patent leather purse, clutched it tighter to her breasts.

—Give us back our money.

—Excuse me?

Perfecto moved forward to grab the crowbar, but Petra held him back.

—I'll smash these windows first, then all these glass jars if you don't give us back our money.

—You listen here!

Estrella slammed the crowbar down on the desk, shattering the school pictures of the nurse's children, sending the pencils flying to the floor, and breaking the porcelain cat with a nurse's cap into pieces. The nurse dropped her purse, shielded her face with her hands. Estrella waited. The nurse began to cry but still had not moved. Estrella knocked the folders which spread like cards on the floor. A lid fell and circled on the floor until it rounded to a complete stop. Estrella held out her hand, palm up.

The nurse stepped forward gingerly and removed the tin box from the top drawer of the desk. She tried three different keys before one slipped into the small lock and unlocked the box and spilled the coins and dollars on the desk and backed away. Estrella counted nine dollars and seven cents. She lowered the crowbar, unable to catch a breath and showed the nurse what she had taken. She did not feel like herself holding the money. She felt like two Estrellas. One was a silent phantom who obediently marked a circle with a stick around the bungalow as the mother had requested, while the other held the crowbar and the money. The money felt wet and ugly and sweaty like the swamp between her legs.

—You should have let Perfecto fix the toilet, she whispered. But it was then that Estrella realized the nurse was sobbing into her hands, her lipstick smeared as if she tried wiping her mouth away. She saw the nurse trembling before her.

Perfecto pumped the gas, then unhooked the dispenser and replaced it on the tank. He gave the old man with a lazy stomach a balled-up five-dollar bill. When he returned behind the wheel, he tapped the gauge with his fingernail and the indicator sluggishly moved to a quarter of a tank. They drove out of the station. The twins looked through the window at the orange Union 76 ball shrinking along with the sun.

The rosary dangled from the rearview mirror. Estrella looked out of the windshield from the backseat of the station wagon. Over the puckering hood, the fluorescent dashes led into the valley and the rows of grapes reamed past them like a spreading paper fan. A few piscadores slowly walked along the belt of the road, their shoulders stooped from carrying the dusk, and they soon became specks of color left behind.

—Did you hurt her? Alejo muttered, repeating it because Estrella couldn't hear the question the first time. He tried to lift his head and licked his flaking lips to lubricate his mouth. His bottom lip bled. The clamor of the muffler scraped the pavement when they hit a speed bump, and his head resonated with powerful blows behind his eyes. It took moments before the pain eased. He cleared his throat. Estrella gently rubbed his feverish forehead with the handkerchief. I need to know.

—They make you that way, she sighed with resignation. She tried to understand what happened herself. You talk and talk and talk to them and they ignore you. But you pick up a crowbar and break the pictures of their children, and all of a sudden they listen real fast.

—Did you hurt her?

—Sweet Jesus, what do you think? Her anger flared. Does it matter now?

—For what? he whispered.

—For what? Estrella asked. For what? For nine dollars and seven cents! Alejo did not understand her sarcasm. He seemed not to understand anything.

—Don't make it so easy for them. The fevers had drained him. He couldn't keep warm enough, and he trembled. Estrella continued to wipe his forehead with the handkerchief, but he grabbed her hand slightly and held it. His eyes welled and became glassy. I'm not worth it, Star. Not me.

—What a thing to say, she replied, forcing her hand away from between his cold fingers.

Estrella looked out again at the valleys and peaks of the mountains they were heading for. She thought of bell peppers. It was odd that this thought came to her. A brisk wind came through the window, and when she inhaled, it awakened her.

She remembered a ranch store. She couldn't remember the town, or the owner of the ranch, or even the particulars of the store, but remembered how the brilliant red and green and yellow bell peppers were stacked like layers of granite stone into small and solid pyramids. The colors became something so completely breathtaking that one had to stop and ask why, why would anyone want to create an incandescent mosaic out of something as nondescript as bell peppers? Estrella wanted to tell the mother, to say, *Mama, take a look at that*, but a woman walked in the store and toppled the peak by removing the top single red one, shiny

152

as new love, and it was as easy to dismantle all that work as it was to kick a can on the road.

—That's a stupid thing to say, Estrella replied, not able to disguise the tone of disappointment. She forgave him because he was sick. *You* don't make it so easy for *them*.

—No. No. No. And he drifted off, his eyes deeply shut. Can't you see, they want us to act like that? Nothing he said could undo what was already done. Nothing could remove the image of Estrella swinging the crowbar and sparks of chipped silver like shrapnel flying in his head.

—Can't you see they want to take your heart? she whispered.

The wagon hummed towards the city of Corazón. Not even Elvis's glitter or the heavenly look of La Virgen held more beauty to Estrella than the red bell pepper.

—She better not call the police, Petra threatened. If she knows what's good for her. She rubbed her forehead and closed her eyes, as if to halt the pounding in her head. She just better not make trouble for us.

—We'll tear down the barn starting tomorrow, right, Perfecto? Estrella asked. She covered Alejo.

—Yes, Perfecto replied. The telephone poles blurred as they travelled the long stretch of paved highway. He could feel the vibration of the engine clear through the stiff leather soles of his shoes, and he felt the heat and the struggle of a car that made no promise. He looked in the rearview mirror and saw night falling and then he saw Estrella speaking to Alejo. She leaned an elbow over the backseat and spoke with him. Perfecto saw her lips pantomiming words, her forehead wrinkling, but couldn't make out what they were saying to one another because Petra had been talking to him.

—The barn? Petra raised her voice at Perfecto.

—We need the money.

—Maybe we can stay in one place, Ricky added, and he sloped on the mother's arm in drowsiness. She raked his sweaty hair.

—Maybe, mi'jo. What do you think, Perfecto? Petra asked.

—Whatever you say. He lied and hated himself for doing it.

The dim headlights shot east to the 281 Exit and on to the signal light at the corner where the Dairy Queen was closed. Perfecto followed the "Hospital" sign down the main boulevard. The storefront shops were locked with grates of steel, and the streelights glowed with a dull luster. A few scattered cars were parked in the Pick 'n Save lot, and a man wearing plastic bags around his waist pulled a two-wheel cart full of crushed aluminum cans and crossed the street right in front of them. One car headed toward them in the opposite direction, and for a minute Perfecto thought it was the highway patrol, but when it drove by, it was only a Chevy with a dented door, and he continued looking out for the signs which led to the Corazón Community Hospital. The twins, having napped, were wide awake and had trouble keeping still. They fogged their breaths on the windows and made finger faces.

They reached the parking lot by nightfall, and Perfecto kept the motor on. The headlights dimmed. He was afraid the battery would die and so dared not turn off the ignition.

—Leave him there.

—Just leave him?

—They'll take care of him, believe me.

—Just leave him?

—Trust me.

—Thanks.

—What?

—Thank you, Perfecto Flores, she repeated, and opened the door. Estrella put Alejo's arm around her shoulder. Perfecto sat behind the steering wheel, the warm hum of engine under his feet. He had given this country his all, and in this land that used his bones for kindling, in this land that never once in the thirty years he lived and worked, never once said thank you, this young woman who could be his granddaughter had said the words with such honest gratitude, he was struck by how deeply these words touched him.

—Hurry.

Estrella emerged from the glass doors of the hospital not knowing quite what to do with the emptiness in her hands. The twins saw her stand there, from the rearview window, just like that, without Alejo. Through the glass, Estrella smiled a small smile when she saw her sisters looking. Then she lifted her arms, her palms up and then spread them wide and the twins watched as she stepped forward and the glass doors split open before her as if obeying her command. Perla turned to Cookie and Cookie turned to Perla. Estrella parted the doors like a sea of glass and walked through and the glass shut behind her and they couldn't for a minute believe what they saw. When Estrella returned to the backseat of the station wagon, the twins fought to sit near her and the mother scolded them and Estrella moved to the middle. The twins nuzzled under her arms. Soon, they were on the main boulevard again and the twins slowly fell into snowlike quiet, shielded and warm and amazed that their big sister had the magic and the power in her hands to split glass in two.

Five

*T*he headlights swerved over the table which stood as they had left it that morning, the cold coffee still in the chipped enamel cup, the stack of plates smeared with hardened egg yolk. The kettle lay on the grate, its base blackened. The car pitched forward and halted. Over the treeline of eucalyptus, transient clouds obscured the moonlight making silhouettes of their faces. Perfecto turned off the ignition and the headlights burned out and the wagon knocked and pinged and was finally silent. They sat in the dark until clouds crossed and the moonlight reappeared again.

The children slept while the mother moved sluggishly to the bungalow. She stopped at the step of the porch to rub the back of her leg, then opened the door

159

and went in. She lit the lantern and the glow of yellow hands appeared to snap the blankets and banish the spiders which hid in abandoned places. The mother stomped on an insect, and scraped it over the edge of the porch with her sandal. She waved Estrella in and Estrella bundled up Perla and carried her into the bungalow while Perfecto carried Arnulfo because Ricky was too heavy for him now, and the mother carried Ricky, heavy or not. Estrella returned to bundle Cookie, and the mother went over to get the stick.

Perfecto slammed the doors of the station wagon one by one. He stared at Petra. Her black wiry hair was undone and it bristled against her neck as she dug the stick into the dirt to retrace the oval ring around the bungalow. She struck the dried stone-packed earth with such force, he could hear the scratch scratch scratch of the stick clawing against the earth.

This was not a time for words; he had to think. He was relieved when she had finished the circle and went back inside and he leaned against the hot hood. He could feel the warmth penetrate the small of his back. He folded his arms over his chest, and clamped his armpits down on his hands to think.

Estrella saw Perfecto standing against the wagon from the bungalow window, the full moon a skin of burns above him.

If Perfecto had a cigarette, he would have smoked it, inhaling the tobacco like a potent drug to tame the panic in the air. There would be no tomorrow, he knew.

He was positive the nurse had called the police. They were probably searching the camps by now. One cigarette was all he craved, just one, but all he had in his pockets were crumbs and lint and half a roll of Certs and the receipt the nurse had given them for services rendered. Without checking his wallet, he made a mental calculation. When they began the day, he had in his pocket all of $9.07. Five dollars gave him a quarter of a tank, and he couldn't decide whether four dollars and seven cents was enough cash to bail out.

What was happening to his instincts? If he were sinking into quicksand, would he not want to save himself? If there was an arrow shot into his belly, would he not think to pull it out? Why had God given him these instincts if they were not intended to be used? Lord, he thought, how tired he was. He wanted to rest, to lay down and never get up, and he pressed his hands to his face.

She thought he was crying.

He rubbed his eyes under his bifocals and folded his arms again. He knew Petra would tell him tonight. Did he think himself fifty years younger to start another family? What a stupid and old man he had become. Stop it. Stop sniffling like a mocoso. Though he wore corrective lenses as thick as soda pop bottles, he was not blind. He knew. But the knowledge was not enough to unloosen himself from the rope of highway.

The mother stood on the porch and glared at Perfecto, one hand fisted tightly.

Perfecto kicked at some pebbles with the toe of his shoe. The maggots appeared and he hadn't the energy to lift his boot and kill them. Think clearly. Remember, the nurse was not hurt, not really. Remember, they had taken only what belonged to them. If, in fact, she had called the authorities, they would've been hauled off to the police station by now. Of course. Of course.

He looked upon the moon's roundness like a quarter, bright as a new dime. Perhaps it wasn't as bad as it seemed. Perhaps the nurse simply reapplied her blood-red lipstick, then drove off just in time to pick up her sons and her sons were probably asleep in their beds right now. Perhaps the nurse was stirring cream into her decaffeinated coffee, the spoon clinking on the cup while her husband watched the late night news. "You won't believe what happened to me today . . . ," she would probably say to him while he lay on the couch, because that is how Perfecto imagined people who had couches and living rooms and television sets and who drank coffee even at night.

Perfecto wanted to load up his tools, a few blankets, some peaches. He couldn't tell whether it was love or simply fear that held him back. His arms folded tighter across his chest, and he dug his hands deeper into his armpits so that they wouldn't move without his permission, so that they wouldn't begin to pack even before his decision was final. He could not wait for the barn and the money and tomorrow. If he left right this minute, without even turning back, pulled the arrow of pain from his belly, he would have a second chance. With four dollars to his name, a chestful of tools, some gasoline, and this old station wagon with a battery ready to die, he couldn't afford time.

Think. Think. Think, Perfecto, you cabeza de burro chingado. The car had cooled and no longer warmed his back and he felt his skin goosebump. He had quit smoking in another life, when his hair was full and black and his children looked upon him as a man who could fix the axles of the world if he wanted to. He looked down at the loose swaying maggots. Perfecto was glad to have given up tobacco. He would have foolishly spent the last few dollars on a package of cigarettes, his desire was such, so overwhelming.

The planks of the floor creaked as they entered bearing the weight of children. The groan of their limp bodies, the comfort of sleeping in a reclining position, dusty blankets under their chins, muddied shoes slipped off their feet. Ricky's ankle red from not having worn socks, Cookie's toenails needed clipping. The buzz of children safely sleeping.

How long would it be before they came to arouse the children? Unleash the dogs? The authorities would come as they did for years, and pull their hearts inside out like empty pockets. How long? Throughout the car ride back to the bungalow, she had asked herself why hadn't she tried to stop Estrella or why hadn't she let Perfecto stop her. It simply came down to this: there was no stopping Estrella, no harnessing the climate of circumstances, no holding back the will of her body. How many times had her own mother warned her, pleaded with her not to get involved with a man like Estrella's real father?

Petra saw Perfecto slamming each car door. One. She stepped down the porch when she saw the stick leaning against the cooking pit and she clasped it like a weapon. She could bare¹ see Estrella's tracings on the ground. Two. In several places, the circle had opened; trampled footsteps had left gaps. All the warnings in the world could not stop her. Three. The scorpions were known to be methodical predators and she scratched the ring with urgency until the ring was at least two inches deep in the soil. Four. When she first became pregnant with Estrella, her own mother blessed her with a kiss on her forehead, then slammed the door shut so final, it never opened again.

Perfecto's back was to her. He leaned on the hood of the car and she wanted to see his eyes. Trust me, she remembered Perfecto saying, but the only trust she had now was in Jesucristo. She palmed her coal black hair back. As she walked up the porch stairs, she let the stick slip from her fingers and fall to the ground. She would make an offering.

Petra had felt eyes all over her. The knot of eyes on the paneled wall glared at her as she slipped the shoes off her children. Then it was the tigereye stones of Jesucristo's eyes which followed her as she kneeled before the statue and lit each candle with a matchbook she kept near its base. The statue, draped in blue robes and crushing a green serpent with bare feet, stood on the elevated middle crate of the Holy Trinity. His removable hands were held out to display the red wounds of crucifixion and the two eyes, surrounded by the half moon of seven candles, gazed through the flames at her. The smoke rose and blackened the ceiling above her candles. Someone sneezed behind the day-blue sheet.

It was no use. She straightened the doily scarf bumpy from the envelope beneath it. The doily had been crocheted by Petra's grandmother and given to her as a gift. The doily was so special, Petra rested Jesucristo on it. She followed the diamond pattern of knotted thread with the tips of her fingers as if caressing a child's face, a jawbone and chin, as if she touched the doily for comfort.

They had whispered among them, las mujeres de la familia, about grandmother and how much of a nervous viejita she was. A curious little sparrow of a woman, with sharp jittery eyes that cut ice. The only thing which calmed her nerves was to sit by the lantern and crochet. When Petra's father was sick, tomorrow came and went and came and went until her father died and tomorrow still came and went and grandmother had crocheted perfect little diamonds through it all. What thoughts had gone through her grandmother's mind as she crocheted, what threads looped and knotted and disguised themselves as prayers? And what had

Petra learned from the trembling fingers which pulled a fine thread into the hook of the crocheting needle with such patience that the stitching was as intricate and as weather resistant as a spider's web? If only Petra was capable of crocheting, if only she could feel the threads slip in and out of her fingers like her grandmother once did, she wouldn't feel as if her own prayers turned into soot above her.

Under the doily lay the documents in the manilla envelope. She slipped the envelope out gingerly and poured out the contents onto her palm. Black ink feet on the birth certificates, five perfect circular toes on each foot, a topography print of her children recorded, dated, legal, *for future use to establish age to enter school, when applying for working papers, establish legal age for rights of franchise, for jury or military service, to prove citizenship, to obtain passports, to prove right to inheritance of property.* Certificado de Bautismos—five of them; a torn and mended Social Security card; Identification card—NOT A LICENSE— She had walked fourteen blocks to get to the DMV, and her picture looked flat and dull and pale as concrete, but the ID was a great relief. Petra often feared that she would die and no one would know who she was. "Remembrance of First Holy Communion" certificate (where was Ricky's—had she lost it?); a thick certificate award given to Estrella for an essay she wrote titled *My Blue Fat Cat*; "Authorization and Certificate of Confidential Marriage"—Personal Data of Husband: He tired quickly. Personal Data of Wife: She was four months pregnant and wanted to change the date, but the man behind the counter said not to worry, he would change it on the record. Married in the town of Santa Ana, county of Orange, state of California. They had to transfer buses twice. They got there five minutes before the office closed, and he held the door open while she went to the bathroom. All the warnings in the world could not stop her.

Petra folded the creases of the documents with the same care she folded a Phillips 66 map, and slipped the papers back into the envelope and placed it back on the altar. She raised herself but couldn't stand without struggling to brace her legs and so she leaned on the crate to support her weight, and the statue of Jesucristo wavered. Her reflexes were no longer fast enough to catch a falling statue; she could almost see the head splitting away from the body before it even hit the wood planks of the floor. The head of Jesucristo broke from His neck and when His eyes stared up at her like pools of dark ominous water, she felt a wave of anger swelling against her chest.

—You okay, Mama? Estrella whispered from the other side of the sheet.

—Go to sleep, she responded curtly.

Petra lifted the head and body of Jesucristo from chips of white plaster on the ground. She was surprised by the lightness of the head, like a walnut in the palm of her hand, and nervously fumbled it upon the neck of the body. Unsuccessful, she replaced the headless statue on the long tread of crocheted doily, crossed herself and kissed Jerucristo's feet. She held onto the head.

Petra licked two fingers and sizzled out the wicks of each candle. She would have liked to keep the vigil burning but was afraid for her children. If one of the candles fell, the blankets would catch, as hungry as fire was, and her children would be incinerated like blazing piñon trees.

She walked to the porch and saw Perfecto leaning against the wagon with his arms folded. As usual, he had his back to her, and he looked into the distance, where the road intersected with the trees. She stared up at the cluster of clouds inching across the moon. The leaves of the top branches had the sheen of polished armor. If only she could crochet a row of diamonds to help her get through to tomorrow. She stared out into the beyond of the moonlight, where the darkness hung like a black sheet. The lima bean in her stomach felt like mesquite burning.

She glanced at the stick cast near the ground scrub. Was it too late to protect the children from the scorpions? Had they already entered the bungalow? Once a weapon, the stick now looked slight and feeble. How could she possibly think to protect her children if such a little clawing insect could inspire a whole midnight of fear? What made her believe that a circle drawn in the earth would keep the predators away? That was all she had: papers and sticks and broken faith and Perfecto, and at this moment all of this seemed as weightless against the massive darkness, as the head she held.

Petra's grasp tightened around the head of Jesucristo. Perfecto stood as quiet as the clouds drifting and she wanted to go see his eyes. If anyone could fix it, Perfecto could.

The smoke of the burning candles made Estrella sneeze and she forced open the window of the bungalow. With all her strength she loosened the swollen pane and the wood scraped against the pulley and she was able to sneak her fingers under and pry it open. The nocturnal air was brisk and welcome after the smothering mesquitelike incense of the room and she inhaled deeply. Not far from the cooking pit, from the unpaved road, she saw Perfecto hide his face with his hands, and his shoulders trembled as if he were crying.

In the hospital room where the vinyl couches were worn and darkened with the weight of people's hours, Alejo's lower lip had trembled and his eyes began to well and his tears caught her by surprise. *Please*, he begged. *Just stay with me for a while*. He was frightened beyond her capacity to comfort him. But the car ran outside, the white fumes rising from the exhaust pipe and the precious gasoline burned and her family waited, and he was where he should be. *Alejo*, she said sternly, *everything's gonna turn out all right. Just tell the doctors*, she said in a voice filled with a combination of tenderness and irritation. She believed it. He would be healed and return to work. It only now occurred to her that perhaps she would never see him alive again, that perhaps he would die.

She felt filthy, the coils of her neck etched with dirt and sweat. Estrella took off the muddied dress as if she wanted to discard the whole day like dirty laundry. Her muscles strained with every body movement and when she had reached for the hem of her dress or pulled her arms out of the sleeves of her muslin undershirt, she felt as if her body had been beaten into a pulp of ligaments and cartilage. She threw the dress in the corner of the room where the children were taught to put their clothes. In the distance, a dog barked then howled. There was a crate in the corner where she had placed her work trousers and she slowly slipped one foot then the other into the pants. The candlelights glimmered a garland of light rays on the sheet which seemed as thin and as transparent as the ears of a desert jackrabbit.

Something shattered on the other side of the sheet, a thud no louder than her own shoe when she pounded it softly on the floor to make sure a spider had not crawled into it.

—You okay, Mama? she asked, opening up her laces and slipping one foot in. She sat near Ricky's pillow to strap on her shoes, tying the laces in double bows. The mother's voice ordered her to sleep and her silhouette moved to snuff out the candle flames with pinches of her fingers. The sheet went blank.

Estrella zippered her work trousers and buttoned up

a clean flannel shirt. She stood and took hold of the lantern, and flipped the corner of the sheet and stepped onto the porch. The mother was already there, staring at Perfecto.

—Where do you think you're going? the mother asked. She held tight to Estrella's wrist. Estrella didn't know and didn't answer.

Then the mother embraced Estrella so firmly, Estrella felt as if the mother was trying to hide her back in her body.

When her eyes became accustomed to the dark and the moonlight paved a worn pathway toward the barn, Estrella knew what to do. The weight of night did not affect her eyesight; her eyes grew like the pupils of a cat to absorb every particle of light.

—Careful with the lantern, the mother yelled to her, The grass is real dry. She cupped her hand around her mouth and called louder to her: It can catch fire! but Estrella did not turn and the mother saw her figure walking unafraid into the darkness, a ball of gold ochre bouncing in the night.

The moon lay flat. Estrella's pace quickened until she realized she was running. She halted abruptly and held up her lantern. A gopher whipped by and disappeared with a rustle into the dry grasses. She could hear the howling of a coyote in the distance, the dogs responding with vicious barks and she continued at a slower pace. The barn loomed before her with its tall shadows and

171

dented weathervane pointing downward. She heard the vane barely squeaking in the whispering breeze, then heard the hinges of the door.

She entered the barn. The inside was dark and dank like the cork of a wine bottle the men passed around on a Saturday night. The light of the lantern wrapped closely around her. At first she was startled by the ticking of the owls' claws above her, then by the sound of fluttering wings and nervous chirping of the swallows. She spoke to her shadow as if she were not alone.

—It's over there, she said and she directed her lantern for a better view of the chain. She tilted her head back. Way above her head, past the loft where some of the birds nested, was a trapdoor to the roof. She could barely see the lines of the moonlight squaring it.

She sat down in the small circle of yellow lantern light and removed her shoes, balled her socks, and tucked them in her shoes as the mother had taught them to do. She was about to turn off the lantern when she realized she had not brought the matchbook with her. She lowered its flame instead, enough to keep the kerosene burning. The blue pilot flame hesitated on its wick, until it wavered reassuringly. Estrella stood up. From her back pocket, she pulled out her bandanna and tied her long hair back with two knots. She spit into her palms, then rubbed her hands against the thighs of her trousers.

—Okay, she said to her other self.

Estrella clasped the chain and hoisted herself up.

There was no turning back now. She pulled her arms to raise her shoulders up until her feet could brace the chain better. The wood above her croaked and cracked slightly from her weight. Bits of splinter wood and dust as fine as ash showered on her and she closed her eyes before it was too late. For a moment the chain swung lightly and chinked against its hook and her grip tightened around the thick links. The taste of soil rolled in her mouth, and a speck watered her eye and she spit. The large thick loops of rust tinkled. The biceps in her arms strained until she was able to wrap her legs around the chain which gave her added support. Her ears hummed.

Her hands were callused and her grip became strong, but her bare feet seemed so vulnerable against the cool, wavering iron. There was no looking down. The coolness tickled her toes. She wrapped the chain between her thighs now and jerked down to raise herself up as if she were tugging on a cord of a bell. She stopped to release one hand and wipe her sweaty palm against her trousers while she hugged tight the chain against her chest with her other. She glanced at the flicks of glow light below, then steered her attention upward to see the door square expanding much larger than she could have imagined it. The intensity of the climb soaked the back of her shirt collar with sweat.

The stench of bird droppings gave the loft a sharp acid smell which cut through the damp hay and alfalfa and dusty nests. The loft was leveled and she tenderly walked across the droppings and fodder which felt almost as brittle and sharp as specks of broken glass hidden under the soft feather down. Her fingers floated in midair and she searched for walls blindly, until she tore into a gossamer cobweb. Something scurried near her foot and she kicked it. By the way it sounded, a lopsided roll, it may have been a wine or Coke bottle, which rolled and flipped over the loft and fell straight down. It took some time before it shattered below, and she realized how high she had climbed. She looked down to see the specks of shattered glass just inches away from the lantern, and for a moment she imagined golden flaming eels dangerously nipping at the straw on the ground. It was so hot up in the loft, her breath struggling against the thin, stale air and she felt her flannel blouse damp and sticky. Her shoes sat near the broken glass with their tongues hanging to the side like dogs panting. She did not stir. Her heart tolled in her chest. She waited for her eyes to become accustomed to the dark. Only after the outlines of walls and floors and ceilings surfaced, did she move toward the trapdoor.

Estrella tried pushing, palms up, but the door only moaned, and she heard the birds somewhere in the barn nervously protesting with incessant chirping. She felt around the edge of the square door to make sure there was no bolt to push out of its notch, no hook that had to be slipped out from its eye. She pressed her back like a shovel against the door and pushed up once again. Again and again until whatever resistance there was gave way to her back. She turned and pushed with her hands and the door swung open against the roof and the swallows flew out from under eaves of the cedar shakes like angry words spewing out of a mouth. Estrella stood bathed in a flood of gray light. The light broke through and the cool evening air pierced the stifling heat of the loft.

She was stunned by the diamonds. The sparkle of stars cut the night—almost violently sharp. Estrella braced her fingers over the rim of the door frame, then heaved herself up into the panorama of the skies as if she were climbing out of a box. The birds pumped their wings in the skies furiously like debris whirling in a tornado, and it amazed her that they never once collided with one another. Over the eucalyptus and behind the moon, the stars like silver pomegranates glimmered before an infinity of darkness. No wonder the angels had picked a place like this to exist.

The roof tilted downward and she felt gravity pulling but did not lose her footing. The termite-softened shakes crunched beneath her bare feet like the serpent under the feet of Jesus, and a few pieces tumbled down and over the edge of the barn. No longer did she feel her blouse damp with sweat. No longer did she stumble blindly. She had to trust the soles of her feet, her hands, the shovel of her back, and the pounding bells of her heart. Her feet brushed close to the edge of the roof and it was there that she stopped. A breeze fluttered a few loose strands of hair on her face and nothing had ever seemed as pleasing to her as this. Some of the birds began descending, cautiously at first, then in groups, and finally a few swallows flapped to their nests not far from where she stood. Estrella remained as immobile as an angel standing on the verge of faith. Like the chiming bells of the great cathedrals, she believed her heart powerful enough to summon home all those who strayed.

Acknowledgments

When I think about the journey to get a novel completed, I can't help but recall all those people throughout the years that have influenced and helped me. It's amazing to remember the times I wrote with Pilar strapped to my back or nursed Francisco while typing. The frustrations and pains of not having the time to let all the stories come out. The absolute realization that I would never complete a project. I think of the years which passed so rapidly.

All this goes up in smoke. Little by little I chipped away at my days until enough time was put aside for the stories. Now I look at my lovely son and beautiful daughter and I wonder where I tucked away all this thing called time.

The food on the table: Thanks to the piscadores, who, with weary bones and hard labor, feed me and you daily. To the U.C. Irvine Chicano Literary Contest; winning first place in the contest and receiving $400 were instrumental in motivating my confidence as a writer.

To the National Endowment for the Arts, for granting me the monies to continue my writing, and to Ms. Mabel Richardson, whose scholarship for "underprivileged girls" helped pay for my undergraduate education at Immaculate Heart College. To my older sister Becky, who never asked—just slipped me a twenty, or took me out to eat during my starving student days. And finally to Eloy, for financially supporting me even during those years we couldn't afford it.

The food of the soul: I want to thank my sincere soul sisters like Sandra Cisneros, who never lost faith in me. What can I say to you, sister, who kept me going in and out of my pregnancies, kept me out of the kitchen, kept my heart still and kept me writing? Terri de la Peña, Mary Helen Ponce, Lucha Corpi, Ana Castillo, Denise Chavez. To Ana María García, who gave up her space for a month so that I might write. Ginger Varney, who is honest and critical. Y tambien a la Elizabeth Gonzales Towers, my comadre de Canada, y la Genet Chavez Gomez de Nueva México, and my homegirls de E.L.A., Irene Hernandez and Suzie Rodríguez, who always have time for me. To my children, Pilar and Francisco. On days when I wake with great fear, they come to me and settle my nerves with a laugh, a kiss, a demand. After that, how could I possibly be afraid of a world they look upon so boldly?

The field of food: Gracias to Las Mujeres de Teoría like María Herrera Sobek (for the long phone and car dialogues), Sonia Saldivar-Hull (Sonia, thanks for your pep talks and advice—You always make me feel my work is very important), Norma Alarcon, Yvonne Yarbo Bejarano, Tey Diana Rebolledo and Debra Castillo. To Raul Villa and Rita Alcala. To Oba, unas gracias fuertes, primo, and a special thank you to my bro, Gary O. To Robert Cantu, who is always so excited to talk about Chicana writers. To my friend D.C., who provided me with my first mountain view. It really was my first and one I will always remember. With gratitude, to my thesis advisors: Judith Grossman, Thomas Keneally, and Gabrielle Schwab. I also gratefully acknowledge Ethan Canin, who encouraged the story, and to my fellow colleagues in the M.F.A. class of 1993, with special thanks to Andrew Tonkovich and Ilene Durst for their careful re-reading of the manuscript, and to Manuel Gomez, my wise compadre and lover of books.

To the blood-red pomegranate seeds of my familia, who always made room in their lives for me: Gilbert, Mary Ann y Alex, Becky y Phil, Serafin y Terry, Frances y Jim, Frank, Ruthie, Barbara y Memo, Carmen and Jack. The Treviño familia—La Señora, y María y Don y Betty y Tony—thanks.

To the oranges and palm dates: the members of the former L.A. Latino Writers Association and/or XhismeArte staff: Victor Manuel Valle, Luis Rodriguez, Marisela Norte, Naomi Quiñonez, Barbara Carrasco, Frank Sifuentes, Joe L. Navarro, and Jesus Mena (a friend to whom I owe tons of love); and to the current members of the Southern California Latino/a Writers and Filmmakers, Inc., my sincere thanks. I also want to extend my love to the Puente students, who have developed intensive workshops in creative writing and see the beauty in themselves and the word.

To leaves, trees, and peaches: To Gabriel García Márquez, who tried in every way to accommodate me after I initially declined the invitation to his storytelling workshop at the Sundance Institute. ¿Qué loca, no? Fortunately, I came to my senses at his insistence.

To the branches that home the birds: To Marie Brown, my agent, who took me on and waited patiently after I broke deadline after deadline promise. To Susan Bergholz, who is a true supporter of our work. To my editor, Rosemary Ahern, who recognized the importance of this story, and kept its integrity intact. To la Marta Treviño, my dear friend, my former roommate, and second mother to my children—many times you took over for me when I felt overwhelmed by parenthood. Gratitude is too small a word to offer you, Marta. Now you have been repaid with your own special gift, José Manuel.

To all the Spirits of my ancestors, of the earth's making, of the heavens which protect and love me, my humble gratitude. To the generosity of mi raza, who love to tell me stories of their lives.

And, of course, to you, Eloy, my gratefulness again. I am always moved and inspired by your love of our people, and your fearless struggles against injustices. Your spirit wraps around me like a lantern light.

We did it. This novel I offer to all of you.